Praise for *The Bolles Series*

Reveiwers have said….

"I just couldn't get enough of this beautiful couple and the hurdles they encountered in coming together."

"A great read, full of steamy scenes and situations, witty dialogues and good secondary characters, and some twists and turns."

"It was an intriguing and engaging reading, very sentimental but also funny and touching. The plot is strong and well developed, flowing beautifully, there are several twists, witty and great dialogues and lovable and interesting characters..."

"I love this author. Her writing is crisp, clear, flawless, and her story-telling is brilliant. I really loved this book from cover to cover."

About the Author

Susie Warren writes heartfelt and passionate contemporary romance with tempting, larger than life heroes and smart, sassy heroines. The stories are set in elite and glamorous worlds and appeal to readers looking for an escape from everyday life by offering jet-set lifestyles and sophisticated plots. Her contemporary series, *The Rosa Legacy* and *The Bolles Dynasty*, feature remarkable, stylish women and the sinfully tempting heroes that challenge them to reveal their secrets, their strengths and their deepest emotions. Susie lives in New York with her inventor husband and their two independent teenagers and at times a world-travelling college kid.

Visit her website, **www.susiewarren.com**, to sign up for her newsletter and a chance to read her next book early, receive information on discounted prices and free books!

The Bolles Dynasty Series

Meet the Bolles Family – Billionaire Oliver Bolles died tragically in a motorcycle accident, leaving his family to deal with speculation around his numerous affairs and rumors surrounding his imploding empire. In the years that follow, his legacy is gradually revealed and his adult children are forced to come to terms with new siblings and past indiscretions.

Book 1: The Forgotten Heiress
Book 2: The Secret Heiress
Book 3: The Chosen Heir
Book 4: The Sheltered Heiress
Book 5: The Rebellious Heir
Book 6: The Protected Heiress

The Chosen Heir

SUSIE WARREN

The Bolles Dynasty ◆ Book 3

The Chosen Heir

Copyright 2015 by Susie Warren
Published by Susie Warren
ISBN: 978-0-9964898-1-2

Second Edition – Rewritten and Revised 2017

Cover design by The Killion Group
Formatting by Susie Warren

For more information on the author and her works, please see www.SusieWarren.com.

For my son

You encourage me each day with your laughter,

kindness and brilliance.

Chapter 1

William Bolles discretely flexed his shoulders, scanning the London ballroom for a sign that the benefit gala would succeed or fail. His sisters had taken a risk by using their father's name to spark interest or curiosity. While he had some allies within the financial industry, most of the wealthy elite viewed him as irrevocably tarnished by his father's misdeeds. It didn't seem to matter that Oliver Bolles had been dead for thirteen years.

His sister, Anna Martin, linked her arm in his and smiled up at him. "There you are. I've been searching everywhere."

He kissed her cheek. "You've put together a brilliant event. The ballroom is at maximum capacity and everyone seems intent on enjoying themselves."

She fidgeted with her necklace. "I had the perfect venue and a dream guest list, but I'm not sure of the auction aspect to this event. What if a particular design doesn't get any bids?"

William watched models showcase the couture gowns that would be bid on shortly. "I'm not an expert in fashion, but I imagine that the gowns will sell."

Anna nodded. "Olivia did a remarkable job of getting the most sought-after designers to participate this evening."

Both of his sisters had overcome many obstacles in their drive to be successful. "It's incredible that Olivia was able to encourage others in the industry to take part." Apparently, the fashion gods didn't hold their father to the same standards as the financial elite.

"It's for a good cause."

"Where is Alistair?" He seldom saw Anna these days without her husband at her side.

Anna flicked her hand. "He's helping sort out a mix-up with the wine. I should check on a few things. Don't look so bored, William. Mingle." She stepped away from him. "I'm surprised you didn't bring a date."

His long-term girlfriend, Angela, had ended their relationship a month ago when he refused to base himself in London. She had no interest in living in Ireland and had given him an ultimatum. He didn't blame her, but had no desire to throw himself back in the dating arena yet. Tonight, with the entire concept of the evening being to bid on one-of-a-kind couture gowns, was not the place to bring a first date. But it wasn't the type of evening that lent itself to being alone, either.

Taking a glass of chilled champagne from a passing waiter, he recognized an old business associate of his father's and raised his glass. He disliked the old boys network firmly entrenched in London, much preferring the chaotic and volatile arena in Dublin.

A woman with long, flowing dark hair and a sexy dress caught his attention. The silky dress she wore clung to her feminine curves and the plunging neckline sparked his interest. She was speaking with Olivia, and he considered whether she was a runway model. She didn't appear to be tall enough for the industry, but she had a high-fashion look to her. Olivia nodded in his direction and the woman headed towards him.

"William?" Her tone was neutral and he smiled to himself. Whoever this was, she didn't idolize him. He much preferred when women didn't shower him with adoring glances. He didn't enjoy the game that his wealth and reputation afforded him. In fact, he met most of his girlfriends on the biking circuit so he didn't have to live up to some unattainable standard.

"Have you been sent with a request from Olivia?" He had no doubt that his sister wanted him to do something.

"Olivia needs you to act as the master of ceremonies this evening. The nanny called to say that Addy fell and might require an x-ray. Fionn rushed home to be with her."

He winced. Olivia's youngest had an adventurous streak and couldn't be easily contained. "Wouldn't it be better to have someone from her organization handle the bidding?"

She glanced away. "It would be impossible to pick one person and not offend the others. You're an outsider to the fashion industry, but a Bolles nonetheless."

"I don't think we've met before." He had no interest in acting as the spokesman for the event, but he couldn't let Olivia down.

She stepped closer to him and held out her hand. Her beauty stood out in a roomful of fashion-conscious individuals, and her deep brown eyes drilled into his soul. "I'm Bridget North. I work as a

3

marketing executive for Olivia's Design House."

He clasped her hand and his body tightened. A physical attraction between them sparked low in his gut. "I'm not a good choice. I can't tell one design from the next."

She looked bewildered for the briefest moment and then recovered, pulling back her hand. "Olivia went to fetch the script for you to review and the teleprompter will have the items listed on it."

He didn't want to easily fall in line with her plans. "I'd hate to disappoint my sister, but..."

Bridget interrupted him. "Mr. Bolles, I know this is sudden, but Olivia desperately needs your help. If the wrong person is put up there, the entire concept could fall apart."

He avoided the spotlight for a reason. "Someone who is a known insider would be better."

She grasped his arm and his heartbeat accelerated. "Olivia asked me to show you the catwalk. Maybe you could decide after you take a look?"

Bridget led him past security and into the area that was set up for the auction and dinner. The technical director approached him and explained the layout and order of events.

Glancing at the catwalk, it looked like countless other fashion shows he had been to over the years. William pushed down a sense of dread. He hated being on stage, under the lights. He was far more comfortable outdoors, not confined in a polite setting with his father's enemies circling.

Bridget pushed her long, dark hair behind her shoulder. "We don't have much time. Can you handle this?"

"Are you planning on assisting me up here?"

She shook her head. "No, I'll be behind the scenes."

Catching her gaze, he said, "I don't know if that's quite fair."

"It was conceived as a solo presentation. There isn't enough time to re-create the flow."

A technician stepped forward and wired him for a microphone.

The beautiful Ms. North went over the event with him and filled him in on all of the intricacies. He was mesmerized by her graceful mannerisms, but forced himself to listen to her instructions. Olivia had put enormous effort into the evening and he wanted it to be successful for her and Anna.

He lowered his voice. "Have a drink with me afterwards?"

Bridget shook her head. "I'll need to help with the closeout."

He smiled at her. "I'll wait."

She nodded and he turned his attention to Olivia, who appeared on the stage.

Olivia looked pale. "Will. Thank you. I'm sorry that this is being thrown on you at the last minute."

He hugged his sister and her body remained stiff. His heart softened. She must be horribly worried about her youngest daughter. "Addy will make a quick recovery."

Olivia wiped away a stray tear. "I'd rather be home, but this event needs to come together."

He touched her shoulder. "The guests will understand if you need to leave for a family emergency."

"Fionn is going to text me when they get to urgent care. If it seems serious then I'll get a taxi."

They discussed the flow and introductions. William rolled his shoulders and allowed others to give him directions, keeping up a lively banter with the guests coming into the room.

When dinner had been served and he was given the signal, he ignored the chaos happening backstage and stepped into the spotlight. The audience gave a loud round of applause and he quieted the room. He read the opening announcements from a screen displayed on the podium, and then he began to introduce each gown by reading a brief bio of the designer and then a description of the actual gown.

Each model walked the runway and guests placed their bids on hand-held devices. Set off to the side was a table recording the bids and keeping track of the purchases. William could hear the final bid amounts in his ear piece.

After more than an hour, the last gown was purchased and he turned over the podium to the director of the charity.

***

Bridget stretched her tight neck and shoulder muscles. As she helped to box up the sold gowns, she hoped William Bolles hadn't waited around for her. She wanted to get back to her aunt's flat and fall into bed. The day had been difficult. It was the fifth anniversary of her mother's death and she had gone to the cemetery early that morning.

She marked the package with the correct bidder number and brought it up front for the address to be properly written on it. She had formed a close friendship with Olivia over the years, but could never quite remove the bitterness she had towards Olivia's father. Maybe it was because Olivia hadn't been raised by him, so Bridget was able to forgive the past, but William Bolles was another story. He had been raised by Oliver and was his chosen heir. It was only natural to assume that he had taken on the man's poisonous morals and behaviors.

Anna walked over to her. "If that was the last gown, then you should head out. Olivia left a short time ago and I have staff to finish the clean-up."

"Thank you. I can't wait to climb into bed."

Glancing around the ballroom, the opulent setting had lost its magic. There were an army of staff taking apart the tables and the runway. William Bolles was nowhere to be seen. He must have decided not to wait after all.

Crossing the hotel foyer, she heard her name called. Turning around, she saw him leaning against a marble column. He looked polished in his formal suit. She had seen his photograph often enough, but somehow he was more powerful and masculine in the flesh. His blue gaze held her steady and she willed her body not to respond to him.

She walked over to him. "I thought you'd have given up on me."

He gave her a charming smile. "Not a chance, Ms. North."

He smoothed down his white shirt and her attention was drawn to his flat stomach and fit body. He kept his dark hair clipped short and she admitted to herself that he would hold most women awestruck.

She wanted to escape his presence, but her innate

politeness wouldn't allow her to simply walk away. "I believe we agreed to one drink?"

He motioned to the hotel bar and she found herself following him to a secluded table.

"If you're hungry, you can order a light meal."

"I'm more tired than hungry. This evening seemed to go on forever."

The server took their drink order and a silence fell over the table.

What could she possibly say to him? He was Olivia's brother and she would never want to offend her employer. "You saved the evening."

He gave her an enigmatic smile. "That is the role of a brother, to step in and rescue the evening when needed."

Bridget adjusted the neckline of her gown. "I'm an only child, so I've never had the luxury of a sibling rushing in and saving the day."

He leaned forward slightly. "Luckily for you, you're rather capable on your own."

She had to be tough and capable because his father had helped pushed her family into bankruptcy.

The server brought over their cocktails and slipped away.

"Have I done something to offend you?" His perceptive question caused her hand to shake and she placed her martini back on the table instead of taking a sip. How could he possibly know her inner thoughts?

She traced the stem of her glass. "Why would you ask me that?"

He reached out and lightly touched her hand. "There's an edge to you when you look at me, but with other people you're friendly and approachable."

She shrugged. "Being famous, you must be used to people knowing who you are and having an opinion about your life."

William took a swallow of his drink. "Ah. So it's nothing personal, but you're not a fan of the Bolles lineage."

She shook her head. "I wouldn't say that exactly. I work for Olivia and know Anna fairly well."

He held her gaze. "It's me, then."

Her stomach plummeted. "No. I didn't care for your father." She wouldn't whitewash the truth for him. His father hurt many innocent bystanders with his lies and manipulations.

He took another swallow of his drink. "My father has been dead for years. You couldn't have been much more than a child when he was alive."

She took a sip of her drink. "I'd rather not drag up bad memories. Suffice it to say that I don't have any respect for the way he lived his life."

She had gone too far; she could see it in the way he held his body rigid. William Bolles wasn't responsible for how his father had lived, yet she couldn't help but focus her bitterness on him.

"You appear to be making a point of some sort. Why don't you come out and tell me what you are accusing my dead father of?"

She shook her head. They were supposed to be having a drink to celebrate a successful evening, not getting lost in some long-ago perceived wrong. "I've said too much. I should go." Bridget gathered her evening bag and stood up.

"You haven't disclosed the issue."

She had made a mistake. He was Olivia's brother

and he would tell his sister about the conversation.

He reached out, grasping her bare arm, and she could feel a spark reach her heart. "Bridget?"

She couldn't hold her accusation inside. "Oliver Bolles had given my father a piece of investment advice years ago. Unfortunately, that piece of advice led my father to financial ruin. I blame your father for playing with other people's lives and not caring about shoddy or irresponsible recommendations."

His gaze narrowed. "Do you expect me to make some type of retribution to your family?"

"Of course not." Bridget pulled out of his grasp. Her mother had died from the stress of it all. The shattered dreams. The bankruptcy. The lies. "It's too late, anyway. The past can't be undone."

William stood completely still. "Maybe you're wrong about the past. You must have been very young."

She crossed her arms. "I'm not wrong about your father. He was a deceitful and horrible man."

Lowering his voice, he said, "Be careful, love. That type of righteous judgment doesn't serve anyone well."

Bridget turned and fled. Why had she let him get to her? She worked for Olivia. Nothing good would come of disclosing the truth to him. She had been careful to hide away her resentment and anger and not let anyone see how much it had shattered her life.

Waiting outside on the street, she pushed away her grief. She needed to get her emotions under control. Going to church early that morning with her aunt had been a mistake. It had created a sense of longing for her mother and made her spend the day thinking about all of the regrets surrounding her teenage years. While it was true that her father had invested all of their savings into a failing golf course based on advice from Oliver Bolles, it was also true that her father had a role to play in the debacle. Thomas North was a dreamer, and even being forced into bankruptcy hadn't changed him.

Bridget flagged down a taxi and tears threatened as she slid into the backseat and gave the address to her aunt's flat. She should have refused to have a drink with William. Instead, she let her curiosity about him make her step outside of her carefully erected boundaries. The mistake would come back to haunt her.

Chapter 2

Bridget stepped onto the tube at Liverpool Street and scrolled through messages on her phone. Instead of taking a seat, she stood in the rush hour crowd and held on to a bar near the door. She considered the various marketing elements that she needed to check on. Getting off at the Whitechapel stop, she waited for a mother with a small child to step out and then moved around them and headed for the exit.

The familiar walk to work eased her nerves. She watched fashionable professionals for clues about the latest trends. Stopping at the restored Victorian factory in London's East End that housed Olivia Grey's Design House, Bridget pushed through the glass doors. She took the elevator to the third floor and greeted the receptionist, Sheila, who was watering the plants.

The young receptionist, a woman with dyed pink hair who wore a tailored short dress, stepped over to the main reception desk and placed the watering can down. "Bridget, Olivia is hoping to catch you first thing. Can you find her?"

Slowing her pace, Bridget asked, "Yes. Is she on the floor?"

Sheila shook her head. "I haven't seen her in fifteen minutes. I'd check her office."

Bridget headed for her cubicle, near a massive set of warehouse windows, and put down her handbag and water bottle. She had a thousand loose ends to deal with, but she took a walk through the cavernous office space, looking for her boss.

It was before eight o'clock, so most of the employees hadn't arrived yet. She found Olivia in her office, a glassed-in area near the center of the building.

Tapping on the door, she waited for Olivia to glance up and gesture to come in.

"Hi, Bridget." Olivia stood. "Have you had coffee yet?"

"No. I just arrived."

Olivia moved to the other side of her office and switched on her coffee maker. "I haven't either, and I thought maybe we could talk over coffee."

"Absolutely." Bridget smoothed the hair on the back of her neck. She loved working with Olivia, and didn't want the awkwardness of an old family resentment to add tension. She had moved past her anger towards the Bolles family years ago. It didn't make sense that it re-resurfaced when she had come face-to-face with his son. Maybe there was something in his look that reminded her of photographs of his father. Her own father had mentioned Oliver many times throughout the last several years. He even kept a framed picture of his brief meeting with Oliver Bolles on his wall.

Bridget perched on the edge of the leather sectional and waited for Olivia.

Handing her a cup of black coffee, Olivia sat down near her. Dressed in white jeans and a pink silk top, Olivia looked relaxed and carefree.

Bridget took a sip of the hot coffee and then placed it on the table. "Thank you. I can't survive the work day without a steady infusion of caffeine. Something tells me today is going to be particularly fast-paced."

Olivia smiled. "There's a ton going on. But I'm concerned about something."

Bridget crossed her legs. "That sounds ominous." She needed her position. Her father relied on her and she had spent the last few years becoming indispensable at Olivia's fashion house.

Taking another sip of coffee, Olivia said, "I'm concerned about The Breen Hat Company falling into bankruptcy."

Bridget closed her eyes briefly and nodded. Her thoughts were jumbled, but she recovered quickly. She had sent out a report last week alerting the top management that the family-owned company based in Dublin would most likely close up shop. Olivia loved their products and Bridget had been scrambling trying to find an acceptable solution. "I know you've used their hats exclusively for years, but we can find an alternative."

Olivia stood and began pacing. "I don't want to use another manufacturer. Breen has perfected their product over generations and the quality and simplicity is a good match for our designs."

Bridget relaxed slightly on the sofa and began to consider the problem. "I don't think we have a choice. My contact at Breen said it's dire. They can't continue to operate."

Olivia formed a steeple with her hands. "I'm considering buying them out or asking my brother to get involved. William is based in Dublin and has rescued several companies from ruin. But I need someone who would be willing to run the business for a period of time."

"Aren't you worried about taking on a company that may not be salvageable?" Bridget didn't want to say too much, but it seemed like a bad idea. She knew first-hand that some businesses couldn't be saved. She grew up watching her father slowly slide into bankruptcy because he had been unwilling to let go of his foolish schemes.

Olivia sat forward and smiled. "Breen makes beautiful hats and has been in business forever. They must have remained in the Stone Age in terms of marketing and reaching new customers. I bet you could help them turn things around."

Bridget shook her head. "I so appreciate your kind thoughts, Olivia. But I don't have any experience rescuing a doomed company."

Without hesitation, Olivia said, "You've helped me with countless launches and we've expanded tenfold in the last five years. I have no doubt that you'd succeed. And you're ready for new challenges. I'd give you a sizable sign-on bonus and stock in the company. It'd allow you to build your CV and make considerably more income."

She couldn't tell Olivia no simply because William might be involved in the purchase. But she wanted to. Taking a leadership role in The Breen Hat Company would be a significant promotion and would allow her more freedom. "What if things didn't go well?"

Olivia rubbed her hands together. "If in the end it

didn't work, then we would find a way to gracefully back out and you'd have a position here. But I don't see that as a possibility."

Bridget stood and tried to look pleased. But on the inside, the breath caught in her lungs. She couldn't allow herself to get caught up in an impossible situation.

After taking another sip of coffee, Olivia smiled. "I'm going to Dublin tomorrow, and I'll let you know how I make out."

"Thank you, Olivia. I appreciate your confidence in my ability." She wanted to say more but held back. "Is that all?"

Olivia stood and walked over to her desk. "I heard from the director of the charity. The gala raised far more than expected. I couldn't have put that together without you."

She nodded. "The event was remarkable. It not only benefitted a great cause, but it brought together the industry. That goodwill will go a long way."

Olivia smiled. "I'm still getting congratulatory texts and messages from other designers."

Walking towards the door, Bridget asked, "How is little Addy? I know Fionn had to leave early."

Tucking a strand of blond hair behind her ear, Olivia said, "She had a hairline fracture in her wrist and came back from Emergency with a small pink cast. She seems to be taking it in stride. The nanny is bringing the girls in after lunch."

Bridget slipped out of her office. She couldn't believe she had agreed to possibly work at The Breen Hat Company. The company was based in Dublin and it'd be an opportunity to make more money and keep a closer eye on her dad. Her infrequent trips to Dublin hadn't been enough lately. But was she ready to leave her well-ordered life in London?

The day passed in a blur as she approved public relations pieces about the event. The photographers assigned to the event had sent their best images, and she directed her assistant to use them in all the social media postings.

At one point, she stopped and examined a photograph of William. He stood at the podium, looking confidant and in charge. His image caused her heart to accelerate. She had grown up despising his father, so it seemed odd that she was fascinated by his son. She barely knew William. Was it possible that he wasn't like Oliver at all?

***

William stood up from the conference table and ran a hand through his short hair. He had returned to Dublin the previous night and was determined to solve the issues at The Dunne Golf Course. He pushed aside an image of Bridget North. Her claims rattled him more than he cared to admit. Over the years, countless strangers had come forward and shared deeply held resentments about his father and how he conducted his life.

He needed to push forward and not let defeat settle into his thinking.

Moving away from the discussion taking place around the table, he looked out at the large expanses of lawn sloping towards the ocean. They were nearly halfway through the renovation of the old golf resort and out of funds.

Years ago, his father had taken him to this shabby

resort and they had spent countless hours learning how to play golf. This course had been a premier location decades ago. It had fallen into disrepair and needed more than essential updates; it needed a complete redesign.

Sitting back down in his leather conference chair, he observed Jeremy trying to justify the recent expenditures, glancing around the room for a lifeline. Unfortunately, no one was coming to his rescue. He expected more of his management team. At the very least, they should stick together.

He kept his voice neutral. "By your own estimations, this project has cost overruns exceeding a million pounds in the prior four weeks alone."

Jeremy loosened his tie slightly. "Yes, well. It wasn't supposed to happen, but the terrain is impossible. You must know that. There is nothing but rock."

"Jeremy, I know this is an impossible project, but you can't allow local vendors to take advantage by charging insane rates."

Alex, his right-hand man, intervened. "With all due respect, William, they have refused to work for a set amount, instead insisting that we pay for machine time. The terrain is rocky and unpredictable."

Purchasing the resort had been a sentimental investment, driven by his need to remember something positive about his father. He couldn't allow it to become the investment that bankrupted them.

Leaning back in his chair, William said, "Gentleman, we knew turning this golf course around was going to take huge sums of money and the willingness to accept risk. And yes, it is out of our usual comfort zone."

Arlo, the member of his team who couldn't be mollified, said, "We could lose our shirts on this deal. It's not worth it. We should cut our losses and move on."

Every one of his managers murmured agreement.

Shaking his head, he said, "No. If we walk away now, we'll lose everything we have invested into this place. We need to change tactics. Let's interview more experts."

Arlo stood up. "It'll muddy the water, Will. They don't know how to make this old relic profitable again. Times have changed. We can no longer count on families to travel to a local resort. They all want to go to the Mediterranean or Belize."

He had overextended his company to acquire the resort, but he would not run from the accelerating costs. He would stay and fight. "We're not trying to reclaim the past. We are attempting to make the course worthy of the European Tour."

Alex said, "It's impossible. They're refusing to even visit until the course is ready."

William shook his head. "We can't allow a golf resort to defeat us. Together, we have resurrected several companies. When we bought this property two years ago, there were a few locals that had attempted to restore it. Get in touch with them."

Jeremy waved his hands in surrender. "That's a bad idea. We bought this property for a song after they lost their life savings on it. I can't imagine they know anything more than we do."

William closed his laptop. "If you've lost faith in the experts, then reaching out to the locals is the next logical step. Go back over the history. Set up a meeting."

Merle said, "One of the three previous owners died recently. I believe another is in America, but I can reach out to Thomas North. He's stopped by a few times."

After a few more minutes of discussion, William moved the conversation to an upcoming cycling event. They rode together on a regional elite amateur team. Their competitiveness and love of cycling provided the perfect background for their management team.

As the meeting ended, William stood and thanked everyone for coming. Arlo and Alex were dressed in riding gear and after trying to cajole William and Merle into joining them, left for a fifty kilometer training ride.

Instead of getting into his vehicle, William placed his bag in the boot and walked the course. They had widened some of the fairways, removed plots of ball-swallowing rough and added intricate sand traps. The result was a faster pace of play considered to be more challenging. The golf course was a beast when the wind howled, but would draw in the elite and beginning players alike.

Checking his phone, he noticed Olivia had texted him: Arriving tomorrow morning for a visit. Private airstrip. Can you collect us?

Everyone else may despise his Bolles lineage, but his sisters were curious about their father and treated his memory with respect. His life would be simpler if his mother could do the same. Instead, she held tightly to her bitterness.

He would sell off more of his assets to keep going

forward. The rolling hills ending at the rough and rocky coastline of the ocean spoke to him. He would play this course frequently and remember his father. Even if his family and most of the world thought that Oliver Bolles, and all of his scandals and lies, were beyond redemption, he would remember the best of him.

Returning home later in the afternoon, William climbed onto his racing bike and headed out to claim his favorite seventy-kilometer circuit. The physical exertion calmed his nerves and allowed him to escape his thoughts about the golf course. The sheer effort of pushing his body past his comfort zone brought him a measure of satisfaction. His empire may be bleeding money, his personal life was superficial and empty, but his body never disappointed him.

***

The next day, William headed out to the private airport to meet Olivia and her daughters. It was nearly two o'clock in the afternoon and he had already put in eight hours of work. He was heading to London in a few days. What could be so important that it couldn't wait until then?

Waiting at the small airstrip, he returned a few calls while watching for the sleek Pilatus PC-12 turboprop to come into view.

His sister and her husband, Fionn, had no shortage of money. They had made smart choices. Olivia's fashion empire was thriving and Fionn had launched his own equity investment firm a dozen years ago and it was booming. William, on the other hand, had taken too many risks in the past five years, and if he wasn't careful, he would soon be bankrupt. The shame caused him to stand up straighter. He'd find a way to succeed.

The Pilatus made a smooth landing and he watched the two-person crew secure the plane. Stepping forward, he saw his two growing nieces, Beatrice and Addy, gracefully walk down the movable steps and run towards him. He tossed Addy into the air, being careful of her recently casted wrist, and laughed at her shriek of delight before turning to Beatrice and gathering her into a tight hug. His nieces were the image of their mother, with their blonde hair and piercing blue eyes.

Olivia stepped down onto the runway in a stylish outfit, but she looked worn out. Hopefully the visit wasn't to warn him of a problem. He had assumed it was merely a chance to catch up before the baptism of Anna's infant son.

He kissed her cheek and when the girls were far enough ahead, asked her, "Is everything fine?"

Olivia smiled at him. "Yes. I was hoping to speak with you about a business concern before you come to London. And it'll be a madhouse with all the events scheduled."

He placed an arm around his sister's shoulders and guided her to his Range Rover. His nieces had already climbed into the back seat and were buckling their seat belts. He opened the rear hatch and took the overnight bags from the pilots.

Climbing into the vehicle, he said, "I have your rooms ready for your stay. What activities do you have planned for the next day or so?"

Addy answered. "Mum said we are visiting a company that makes hats and then we will collect samples of lace."

He glanced over at his sister and she smiled. "Tomorrow's plans. Let's go back to your place and chat."

William asked his nieces about their studies and hobbies on the short drive back. Most of his inquiries were met with giggling and he kept up a teasing banter with them.

Olivia asked, "Can you slow down around the curves?"

He downshifted. "Are you not well?"

Olivia shook her head.

His housekeeper, Mrs. Blake, greeted them at the door and said she had set up their favorite tea and sandwiches on the back terrace. Olivia took a call from Fionn and joined them a few minutes later.

The girls chatted amicably and then disappeared the moment their tea was consumed.

"They're growing up, those two. How old are they now?"

Olivia took a sip of her tea. "Seven and eleven. I would have thought you would remember that, as you never miss a birthday."

Tension wound its way through his shoulders. He had a few things to take care of before he headed to London. "You're a wonderful mum, Liv."

She put her cup down. "It's a good thing, as I'm expecting a baby in January."

Delight swept through him. His sister and Fionn were made to be parents. Their dedication to the girls never faltered. "Fionn must be over the moon."

Olivia was nothing like his mother. He wished Olivia's children could count toward his allotment of

23

future offspring. But Diane had made it clear that she had no interest in her husband's "mistakes" as she termed both of his sisters. It was the reason he rarely saw his mother.

His sister's face lit up. "Yes. He's thrilled."

He smiled at her. "Shouldn't you be home resting?"

Olivia smoothed down the edges of her skirt. "It's early in the pregnancy. I'll have plenty of time to rest later on." She sat forward. "I wanted to talk with you about a business opportunity."

He raised his eyebrows. He and Olivia rarely spoke about business. She was firmly enmeshed in the fashion world and focused on designs or culture. "I'm all yours."

Olivia stood up and began pacing. "Do you remember meeting Bridget North at the event this past weekend?" Olivia paused and waited for him to nod his head. "She's a marketing genius and alerted me that my favorite hat company in Dublin is about to go out of business."

He remembered Ms. North and her sharp tongue. Where was Olivia heading with this? "Many of the garment-centered businesses can't compete with the lower labor rates abroad."

She looked at him. "It's an old family business that has been in existence for a hundred and fifty years. They make the most beautiful hats. I can't imagine them disappearing."

She wanted him to save the company. "Have you asked Fionn about it?"

Her voice rose with excitement. "He's not interested in taking on a small, family-owned business in Ireland. But you've based yourself here and you have a management team that is skilled at turning around failing companies."

He tempered his words. "Liv, some of the companies I've purchased are no longer in existence. In order to become profitable again, sometimes re-structuring works but if not, at times the company has to be broken apart and sold for the assets."

Olivia remained silent and looked at him. She expected him to wave a magic wand. It wasn't that simple. Companies went bankrupt for many reasons.

He stood up. "It doesn't make sense to purchase one of your suppliers to keep them around so you don't have to find a new source."

She crossed her arms. "You don't understand. They make custom women's hats that can't be found elsewhere."

He couldn't take on another failing business. The golf resort had enough problems. "Do women even wear hats anymore?"

"What?" Olivia blinked at him.

William shrugged. "It's a fair question. None of the women I've dated have ever worn a hat beyond maybe a baseball cap."

"Maybe you're dating the wrong women." It often came back to this.

He ran a hand through his hair. "I can't take on a failing hat company. The garment industry in Dublin is complicated at best. I don't have the experience to know what to do with a hat company."

She pulled out her chair and sat back down. "I disagree. There has been a resurgence of skilled shops. You understand numbers, Will. How hard can one small company with less than fifty employees be to manage? It is ten minutes from here."

The timing was wrong for him. "There's a steep knowledge curve in each industry."

Olivia waved a hand. "Bridget North is willing to take on running the company. She understands marketing, knows the industry, and she's from Ireland."

He had no interest in working with the uptight marketing genius. "Does she have experience running a company?"

Olivia shook her head. "She's well-educated and savvy. I'm sure with some mentoring she'd be up to the task."

The housekeeper, Mary Blake, came in and asked, "Can I clear the dishes?"

William looked at her. "There's no rush. Don't you normally take a break in the afternoon?"

His kind housekeeper hesitated and straightened her apron. "The girls want to help with dinner so I've sent them to change and thought I'd take care of this before I lose track of time."

Olivia smiled. "Are you sure they won't become a nuisance for you, Mrs. Blake?"

The housekeeper stopped gathering the tea items for a moment. "I selected the ingredients for dinner with them in mind."

William stood up and opened the door to the house for his housekeeper who was carrying a tray loaded with dishes. "Thank you, Mary."

He needed to find a way to distract his sister. Leaning on the low stone wall surrounding the terrace, he asked, "Have you spoken with Ms. North?"

His sister glanced out over the garden. "Yes."

He'd have to tell her no. "Olivia, I want to help, but before I decide to purchase a company, I review the financials, possible assets, and current market trends."

Olivia touched her flat belly. "I'm inclined to purchase it myself, but I'm worried about taking on too much."

He looked away. She was a force of nature, but she was right: with a pregnancy and then an infant, the timing was wrong. "Maybe the hat company will limp along for another year and then you could think about it."

She touched his arm. "I scheduled a meeting for tomorrow. They're within days of closing the shop."

His mind raced through various possibilities. "What's the name of this company?"

Olivia smiled. "The Breen Hat Company. Have you heard of them?"

Her hopeful look pierced his resolve. "No. I can't say that I have."

Giving him a pleading look, Olivia said, "Please, William. Have Alex or Arlo take a look at the company and see what can be done."

He smiled at her. "I will. But don't get your hopes up."

She stood up and hugged him tightly. "I'll go rest until dinner. Is it fine if I ask Bridget to take the ferry over? Can you meet her in the morning?"

The idea of spending time with Bridget North irritated him. "I can pick her up. But I can't make any promises about Breen until I visit and go through their financials. And I'm not sold on Ms. North."

William headed to his office and, instead of dealing with other pressing business issues, he delved into the information available on the family-owned hat company. His own business network was in trouble and he needed to focus on stemming the flood of money, not taking on more of a burden. Somehow, he'd make it work. But mentoring Bridget North was not in the cards.

Chapter 3

The next morning, he stood near the ferry departure ramp waiting for Bridget. He placed himself near a brick wall so he would be conspicuous. Would she mention her parting words to him, or pretend it never happened? William relaxed his tense muscles and made an effort to let go of the incident. He had been drawn to her and asked her to have a drink. Unfortunately, she had revealed that she had no respect for his father or the way he had conducted his life.

He should have been prepared for the verbal assault; it had happened countless times over the years. How could Ms. North possibly know anything about his father? He had been dead for thirteen years, and Ms. North couldn't have been more than a child when he was alive.

Bridget got off the ferry, and in an unconscious gesture, pushed her long brown hair away from her face. She wore a stylish grey fitted dress with a small belt, and he remembered why he was drawn to her. She was sexy in a slim, graceful way and looked approachable, even friendly. Only he had discovered that the polished Ms. North had a sharp tongue and a heightened sense of fair play. She'd made it quite clear she had not approved of the caviler way that his father had lived his life. No doubt that judgment extended to him, as well.

***

Bridget turned on her four-inch heels and looked down the plank. She caught sight of William Bolles leaning against a wrought-iron fence and sternly reminded herself not to show the slightest reaction. His image had been seared into her mind. He was charming and daring. For some odd reason, she hadn't wanted to reject him. He had been unexpectedly good-natured. But he had been raised by Oliver Bolles and undoubtedly had issues with integrity and the truth.

Bridget had had enough of fly-by-night dreamers who only cared about the next big scheme. Even now with her mother gone, she was supporting her father in a crappy little studio flat over a pub. She could barely afford her own living expenses in London while trying to save her father. She had Oliver Bolles to thank for the years and years of hardship and struggle.

She walked over to him and held out her hand. "Mr. Bolles, it's lovely to see you again."

He rose to his full height and grasped her hand, saying, "Will, please. It seems we'll be spending the next couple of hours together in a discovery process."

She removed her hand and grudgingly said, "Will."

"Mr. Bolles is a tad formal for someone who shredded my offer of a meal."

Her gaze shot up and she met blue eyes full of curiosity. "I'm not sure I remember it quite that way."

"Your exact words were I'm not wrong about your father. He was a deceitful and horrible man." His gaze narrowed. "It's curious that you work for my sister Olivia Grey Bolles. Obviously your condemnation of the Bolles family doesn't extend to her."

She had expected him to pretend that the conversation never happened, not address it word for word. She had been too harsh. But her resentment lingered around the edges of her subconscious, no matter how hard she tried to forget the past. Her father was a destroyed man because of Oliver Bolles. And now by some twist of fate, she was pushed into working with his son. She couldn't easily say no to Olivia. Her boss desperately wanted to see The Breen Hat Company survive, and while she didn't want to work with William, the opportunity it presented was too good to pass up.

"I was having an off night. But I shouldn't have said those things about your father. It happened a long time ago and I've moved on."

***

He acknowledged to himself that he should move on. It wouldn't serve him to hold onto her unkind words. Unfortunately, his father had his faults. Bridget had sexy curves that would tempt any man, but her razor-sharp tongue would cause any mere mortal to bleed.

He had too many skeletons in his closet. Most, if not all of them, were his beloved father's misdeeds or lies, but he didn't need to invite in a righteous marketing executive that had no idea of how difficult it was to carry the Bolles name. Taking on the family business and inheritance had made him a target for all those who hadn't dared to challenge his father when he was alive, but, now that he was gone, had no remorse when attempting to tarnish his reputation.

William stepped back as she raked her gaze over him. She readjusted her overnight bag on her shoulder and waited for him to lead the way. He liked the look of her. She dressed in high fashion, but it was understated and polished instead of outrageous. Her face held a trace of cosmetics, but it was subtle. He couldn't allow her physical attributes to sway him, though. She would be too much trouble.

He met her gaze and lowered his voice. "I appreciate the apology of sorts, but if we are to work together, even briefly, I'd like you to keep your opinions about my father to yourself."

She raised her eyebrows in surprise. "I can't imagine a discussion about your father will come up. But you should know, I always tell the truth. Even if it's difficult to hear."

He ran a hand through his hair. "The ability to tell the truth is an asset, but giving unsolicited and unfounded opinions about something you know nothing about is not."

He led her to his metallic Porsche and helped her fit her overnight bag in the small space that was designated as a back seat.

Closing her door after she climbed in, he walked around the low sports car. He brought the engine to life and tried to block out her enchanting perfume. Being in the fashion industry, she must know how to make herself irresistible. But he'd resist her.

Bridget turned to him. "Have you looked into the history of The Breen Hat Company?"

He glanced over his shoulder and pulled out into

traffic. "I did some research last night. Olivia arrived yesterday and shared her idea for saving the company."

Bridget tucked a lock of hair behind her ear. "I've had several conversations with the owner, Patrick Breen. He hoped Olivia would be tempted to purchase the company."

His sister could be focused and persistent. "She does love the product."

Bridget glanced down at her hands. "Yes, but it does seem like too much to take on, running a failing company in a different country."

He shifted gears. "Not to mention the economy is not favorable to Irish products when labor overseas is far cheaper." He should rein in his opinions. He needed to approach the company with an open mind.

Bridget nodded. "There's a tremendous amount of tradition and culture related to the garment industry. When I was growing up, everyone's grandmother was a seamstress and the skills were something to be proud of."

He maneuvered the Porsche into another lane. "We'll be there in a few minutes. It's important that we don't give away our thinking. We need to ask tough questions and find out why they are bankrupt."

Her voice softened. "They're probably going bonkers. They're about to lay off employees that have been with them their entire working life."

They couldn't afford to mix emotion in with business decisions. "Where is the sharp-tongued truth teller?"

Bridget crossed her arms. "Excuse me?"

He was being a tad unfair but couldn't resist. "I

thought you liked to challenge others and insist on knowing the truth."

"I know the truth. The company is failing both from circumstances beyond their control and an unwillingness to try new strategies. I'm familiar with their presence in the marketplace and have visited the factory before." Her logic appeased him. He liked that she was willing to stand her ground.

He needed to rein in his reaction, but said, "So you are only merciless while trying to make a point about the Bolles name?"

After a slight pause, she said, "I thought we'd covered this already. I'm sorry if my comments the other night offended you."

He didn't want her apology. But he also didn't want the complication of taking a look at The Breen Hat Company. He needed to focus on his other investments.

The faster she was back on a train to London, the better it was for both of them. "You're not on a mission of discovery, but one to convince me to invest?"

"Olivia thought I could help you understand the company and the market. But I do feel sympathy for the employees. They must be feeling dazed and anxious."

He slowed for a red light. "I feel badly for the employees. But if we are to purchase the company, it has to be because we think that it can be turned around. I don't want to elongate the eventual demise of the company."

She turned towards him. "I don't work for Breen, but I'm sympathetic. I'm hoping that some type of agreement can be forged that'll allow them to keep operating."

William pulled into the parking area for employees. "I understand your sympathy, but at this point, it'd be irresponsible to offer hope to anyone. If we can't see a way to bring this company back to profit, then we shouldn't get involved."

Olivia wanted him to act as the knight in shining armor and had selected Bridget to further the cause. But he wouldn't allow anyone to dictate his business choices. If he couldn't find a reason to invest, he'd walk away. Even if his sister was momentarily upset.

He waited for Bridget to climb out of the car and watched as she straightened her dress and placed her large handbag over her shoulder.

"I'm locking the car, if you want to leave anything behind."

The top of her head barely reached his shoulder. "My bag has a notebook and relevant files."

He gestured to the side entrance of the building and followed her. Stepping inside the factory reminded him of Old Dublin. The brick building had to be two hundred years old, and the factory-style windows were placed high enough that air could flow, but employees couldn't see out. Beyond the reception area, he could see a vast cavern of sewing equipment and other machinery. From his research last night, he knew there were more than fifty employees that counted on Breen to keep operating.

***

The factory floor was darker than she remembered. Maybe it was the absence of lighthearted banter. The employees were busy at each station and didn't look up from their work. It'd be so much better if William could see everyone at their best. While she hoped the company could be spared, moving back to Dublin didn't bring her any real happiness. She had created a life for herself in London, far away from the issues that had plagued her parents.

William greeted the receptionist and said, "We have a meeting with the owner, Patrick Breen."

The woman nodded and picked up an old, outdated phone and called upstairs.

After a brief hesitation, she said, "Mr. Breen is expecting you. Do you know the way?"

Bridget smiled. "Thank you, Frannie. It's good to see you."

"Hello, Bridget. It's wonderful to see you, dear."

Walking through the wooden gate, Bridget waited a moment for William.

She led him through the shop floor, paying attention to the marked pathway on the cement. It was obvious that the employees knew of their visit and greeted them as they passed by.

William stopped and inspected a bowler hat. The man at the station was shaping the hats and said to him, "It's one of our top sellers."

"I can see the fine workmanship." He placed the hat back on the stack.

He was difficult to understand. He treated the employee with respect; he hadn't come off aloof or unconcerned. But judging from their discussions so far, she was convinced he wouldn't invest. He'd look for a token reason to refuse Olivia. The employees here needed a lifeline.

At the far end of the factory, she led him up a

steel staircase. She could feel his gaze on her as she walked in front of him. Was he attracted to her? Reminding herself not to be insane, she hurried up the stairs.

When they reached the fireproof steel door at the top of the stairs, William placed a hand on her arm and turned her to him.

"Before we meet with the owner, I want to remind you not to give anything away. We're here to gather information."

The breath in her lungs stilled. He was standing much too close to her. What was it about him that caused her body to react? In the fashion world, she came into contact with attractive men all the time, and she'd feel nothing. Yet a Bolles descendant, whom she despised for his lack of morals, caused her to become breathless. She needed to focus on his flaws, not his captivating, intense look.

Their gazes were locked in a silent duel of wills and she became aware of his breathing.

"I get it." She looked away and waited for him to step back.

He adjusted his tie. "Not every business can be saved."

Stepping abruptly to the side, she wrenched the door open and walked into the dingy space. Looking around the outdated office, she knew William would not be impressed. Hopefully, he'd concentrate on the products being made downstairs.

He whispered to her, "The décor reminds me of factories in operation fifty years ago."

Patrick Breen came out of one of the conference rooms to greet them. He was in his fifties and had worked at Breen since he was twelve years old.

"This is Olivia's brother, William Bolles. Allow me to introduce the owner, Patrick Breen."

She waited for them to shake hands and exchange a few pleasantries.

Patrick said, "I thought we could assemble in the conference room, and then call in different employees as you have questions."

***

William stepped into the cramped conference room. The atmosphere surrounding the shop reminded him of distress. Books and trade magazines were stacked in piles on the floor. At least it had windows with a view of the street. He had to separate his tendency to want to solve problems from taking a straightforward look at the business. If the owners were incapable of embracing change, it'd be difficult to salvage the business.

Looking at the various products displayed on the table, he said, "This visit is not about the quality of the products you produce. It's understood in the marketplace that Breen makes superior hats. It's about the financials and how willing you are to change your business practices."

Patrick Breen rubbed the back of his neck. "We're open to re-positioning the business, Mr. Bolles. We want to protect our employees."

"Their willingness to change and take on new roles within the company will be crucial." It was better that he didn't soften the blow. If they expected the business to go forward, then they must accept change. Leaving everything the same and adding money wouldn't save them. "Let's get started. Can I see your latest Audit? And I'd like to speak with the person in charge of handling daily transactions and get a list of outstanding accounts."

He pulled out a chair at the end of the table and opened his laptop.

Patrick awkwardly stood by the door. "In that case, I'll leave you to speak with the bookkeeper."

"I'll call you when I'm ready to speak with you." The owner nodded and left the room. Did Patrick Breen not get involved in the financial life of the company?

The bookkeeper, a woman in her sixties with a trim figure and glasses on a pearl necklace, came in with a large binder that had hand-written account statements.

He greeted her and then asked, "Are these statements in the computer?"

She shook her head. "No, we reply on a manual system and then when the customer pays, we record the payment in the computer."

They couldn't rely solely on paper statements. "How do you know what customers owe on any given day?"

She tapped the book with her fingers. "We total up the amount once a month from this ledger."

"Bridget, can you total this? And get the director of marketing." He handed her the book.

He turned to the bookkeeper. "If you'll stay for a few questions?"

He spoke with her without pressing too hard. It was obvious she was conscientious but not particularly savvy about technology.

After speaking with the marketing manager, an

image of the company began to form in his mind. They hadn't stepped into the new millennia. They were doing business as they had decades ago. It wouldn't be that hard to assemble a team to revamp their business practices. It was far easier than solving the issues at the golf resort. Within a year, the Breen Hat Company could be bringing in a profit.

Watching Bridget with the employees, he saw that she put them at ease while asking tough questions and leading them down a certain path. She could be an asset to his management team, for this project and the golf resort.

He and Bridget spoke with Patrick Breen at length behind closed doors and were satisfied with his responses.

When William offered an influx of currency and the technology to revamp their business practices for seventy percent of the company, Patrick stood and offered his hand.

William stood and said, "Before we shake hands, do you want a few days to talk over the deal with a trusted advisor or your spouse?"

Patrick rubbed the back of his neck. "No. We need this lifeline. Without it, I'll have to close."

William shook his hand. "There is an upward climb ahead of us. But after everything I've seen today, the company has enormous potential."

Patrick adjusted his glasses. "Can I announce the acquisition today?"

"You can call together your employees and reassure them that an acquisition is being negotiated. We should coordinate a formal announcement with a Public Relations firm, so don't give any specific details."

The Breen owner clasped his hands together. "I can't thank you enough."

"My attorney will be in touch in the next day or so with the legal agreements, and then I'll instruct my bank to wire enough funds to cover your immediate requirements. Bridget and I will work on an overall transition plan and one of us will reach out to you in the next week."

Patrick turned to Bridget. "I can't thank you enough for everything. I can't believe we'll stay open."

Bridget smiled and patted his shoulder. "Olivia will be relieved."

Leaving the office, William gestured for Bridget to come with him. He walked with her through the shop without stopping and out to the parking lot.

Standing by the car, Bridget turned to him. "William, I can't believe you decided to purchase seventy percent of the company without thinking it over."

He smiled. "It wasn't a hard decision. They have a quality product and name recognition. They need to be brought into the current economy. Let's discuss the transition over lunch, and then I'll drop you at the ferry."

He took her to The Brazen Head, a favorite pub of his in Dublin. The pub overflowed with business professionals, but he was recognized as a regular and the server found a table for them.

"Have you been here before?" It was a well-known establishment and a favorite of locals.

She shook her head. "I spent the last nine years in

London."

"You left Dublin before University?" He wanted to know more about her.

Bridget opened the menu. "Yes. My mother had been ill for years, and I have an aunt in London who helped me get into a business school there. She works in fashion, so I had access to internships and opportunities I wouldn't have had otherwise."

"How about your papa?"

Bridget sat back in her chair. "He lives in Dublin and I visit him often."

The server came and explained the specials. Bridget ordered lemon and garlic chicken. He ordered a stout and the beef stew.

"I made the offer today contingent on you working with me for a year."

She met his gaze. "Olivia mentioned the possibility, but I didn't think you would invest. It's risky taking on a failing company. And I'm not entirely sure about relocating to Dublin for a year."

The server put their drinks in front of them.

The move to running Breen would be a promotion for her. "How serious are you about saving the Breen Hat Company? Olivia gave me the impression that she wanted you on the project."

Bridget folded her hands in her lap. "I can help for a few weeks and then you can hire someone appropriate."

The server delivered their meals then disappeared into the crowded pub.

"I'm not willing to take on a company in the garment industry without a solid commitment from you. Olivia mentioned a year and then you would be offered another position within her company."

A strained silence sprung up between them.

She repositioned her pendant necklace. "I can't walk away for a year. All of the contacts I have built will be lost."

Bridget already had a rapport with the Breen employees and had the skill set to drag them into the present. "You've a decision to make. I'll let Olivia know you're considering it and we can have a chat in a week. I'll be in London for my nephew's baptism."

She placed her fork down. "I don't want to relocate to Dublin. And frankly, we may find it difficult to work together."

He wondered if she had a serious boyfriend that Olivia didn't know about. Maybe that was why she seemed reluctant to come back to Ireland?

"You have a difficult choice ahead of you." He'd find her price point and exploit it.

He finished his stew, giving her a chance to think about the opportunity.

Bridget took a few bites of her meal.

He took a swallow of ale. "The position will have a significant sign-on bonus and an increase in salary. When you return to London, the experience of running a company will only help your career. And it can't be a bad thing to have the founder of the company in your debt."

***

Bridget had an empty feeling in the pit of her stomach. Why did he want her to work at Breen? He could hire an experienced businessperson who'd be grateful for the work.

She wanted to help Olivia, but she couldn't spend

the next year in Ireland. There were too many painful memories. It'd break her heart to see her despondent father each week instead of a few times a year. He had never changed and continued to dream of making it big. She could barely hold it together as he spoke about his next scheme. He was even talking about the dreadful golf course. They had lost everything to those dreams.

She took a sip of water and tried to relax her tense shoulder muscles. "I'll need time to think about it. Breen makes a wonderful product, but I don't know if I'm suited to spend a year in an old-fashioned factory. I've never been excited about the production process. I'm much more interested in helping to build a line or figuring out new ways to reach customers."

He smiled. "If I take on Breen, it won't remain in the dark ages. I'm offering you a position on my management team. Breen would only be one project; there are several other companies."

She took a small bite of chicken and thought about his offer. There was resistance in every cell of her body. Her rational mind knew it was a good offer, but she couldn't escape her emotional reaction to putting herself back in harm's way.

"You'll have the opportunity to travel back to London frequently."

A rise in salary would get her father a nicer flat in a better neighborhood. She wouldn't have to worry so much about him. But could she live in Dublin and keep her sanity?

Bridget pushed her long hair behind her shoulder. "Why do you want me to work for you? There must be so many more qualified candidates."

He placed the glass bottle on the table. "You've a natural rapport with people, and you're intelligent enough to see the bigger picture. Olivia believes in your marketing ability. There are some individuals that are brilliant with numbers, but can't effectively deal with employee issues. My guess is that Breen will need a considerable amount of hand- holding in the coming months. I'm not inclined to be that involved."

She met his gaze. Was he complimenting her? Or did he expect her to deliver bad news to the employees?

She titled her head. "You might find that I'm more sympathetic to the employees than I am to you."

William checked his phone. "Maybe you'll find that you agree with my thinking."

"I won't agree to lay off a large part of the workforce at Breen." Her spine straightened as she said, "If you intend to pay me an exorbitant salary and have me do your dirty work, then you'll be disappointed."

"Ms. North, you have such an imagination. I'm not sure what you are referring to in terms of dirty work, but I'm guessing you mean firing employees? Rest assured, I have no problem firing people myself. But I have no interest in holding an employee's hand and gently encouraging change or growth. That would be your domain."

He signaled for the check. "You've a ferry to catch. I'll see you in exactly a week and you can give me your answer."

Bridget allowed him to guide her through the hectic restaurant and out onto the street. She guessed he preferred a valet service, but seemed at ease retracing his steps back to his parked Porsche. This time he opened the door for her, and their bodies touched briefly as he helped her into the low sports car. She couldn't wait to escape his presence and be safely on her way back to London.

They barely spoke on the short drive to the station, and he double-parked near a taxi stand. He leapt out and retrieved her overnight bag from the back seat.

"Safe travels, Ms. North. Until we meet again." He smiled at her and then abruptly left her standing there. She didn't allow herself a final fleeting glance at him and instead walked into the station and looked up at the departure board.

Taking a deep breath, she attempted to settle her nerves. She should feel pleased that she had a choice, but somehow it didn't feel like much of a choice. Olivia would be clamoring for her to take the position, and it would be massively difficult not to accept the higher salary. She had been struggling for so long that it almost felt too good to be true. But what would she have to give up for this gift?

Chapter 4

The following week, William flew his Cessna Mustang solo for the short flight from Dublin to London. Flying by himself, even on short flights, allowed him to fully relax. The trip was meant to combine business with pleasure. Not only would he be attending his young nephew's baptism, but he also scheduled a few meetings meant to bring in capital to his struggling investment group. Having the Bolles name had limitations, but it also opened doors to a number of extremely wealthy individuals in London. He would need to be careful or his brother-in-law, Fionn, would know that he was starved for cash. It limited whom he could approach.

An image of Bridget permeated his usually focused mind. He hoped he wasn't making a mistake by hiring the young but rather savvy marketing executive. The issues at the golf resort needed to be solved so he could stabilize his burgeoning investment company. His shareholders were patient, but two years of losses was enough. He had no intention of going in front of the group in nine months and having to explain another loss.

The crew at the small, private airstrip met him on the runway. They handed him the keys to his rental car and would take care of all the required checks of the aircraft.

"We'll see you in few days, Mr. Bolles."

He traveled with only a briefcase, and thanked the crew before heading to the car.

Driving into London, he thought about his sister, Anna. He had yet to meet his infant nephew, Oliver Martin, Anna's second child and now the namesake of his dead and disgraced father. Why would his sister saddle her son with their father's name? His mother had been livid. It brought back the heated scandal of his father's infidelity with Elizabeth Harris. But Anna and Alistair hadn't worried about any of that. They moved forward and named the boy Oliver.

At least his mother had refused to come; that would make the occasion a little easier to bear. Having Diane dressed in all black and standing off in the distance didn't help family relations. Mostly, his sisters felt sympathy for him, but occasionally would insist he do something about his bitter and vengeful mother. And Anna's mother, Elizabeth Harris, was not above creating a scene. Olivia was the only one who didn't have to deal with insane relatives.

William managed the rush hour traffic and parked in an underground garage. His flat in London had been recently renovated and he was looking forward to seeing the work. He had purchased the flat five years ago when Anna had married. It made sense to have a home base in London, but he had rarely used it.

His assistant had come to London a week ago and unpacked his clothing and cycling equipment. He also made sure the flat would have a chef on call and a housekeeping service coming daily. He had planned to have a few dinners while in London and hoped to be able to introduce Bridget North to his contacts.

Opening the ornate door, he glanced around the modern space. The architect had removed walls and opened up the now light-filled space. It was decorated in muted grey tones with large black-and-white photographs adorning the far walls. The spectacular view was London sprawled out in front of him. It was flawless.

He changed into cycling gear and carried his bike onto the service elevator, getting off on the main floor. The doorman nodded to him as he walked through the lobby of the exclusive building. Stepping onto the sidewalk, he attached the front wheel and checked over the frame before putting on his helmet. He ignored the professionally dressed stream of Londoners glancing at him. He needed to expunge the excess energy from his body. Checking his power meter to start the circuit, having mapped out a fifty-kilometer ride through the city and beyond, he climbed onto the bike and merged into traffic. He had three hours before he was expected at Olivia's for a family dinner.

***

Bridget checked the time again. It was after nine o'clock at night and she was trying to finish the last of her projects. She had met with Olivia twice in the last few days and decided it would be unwise to refuse her offer. The company was giving her a generous bonus for her willingness to assist with The Breen Hat Company and a contract for her return in a year.

It didn't make sense that she wanted to refuse the offer. The money would be enormously helpful and would allow her to purchase a small cottage for her father. It'd allow him to finally have some security.

Olivia and her aunt had assured her that the career move she was making would only enhance her CV. So why was she so reluctant?

It had to do with William Bolles. He was so sure of himself. He only had to snap his fingers and everyone acquiesced. She didn't want to be put in the position of answering to him. It was for a year. She should be able to survive and she planned on keeping herself busy.

Her mobile buzzed. Are you free to meet for a drink? OXO Tower Bar at 10:00.

Bridget sighed deeply. She would be finished, but had no desire to meet William Bolles for a drink tonight. Instead she wanted to feel sorry for herself. Go home to her aunt's flat and eat ice cream from the pint container. Instead, she'd be an adult.

She texted back, See you then.

Finishing her work, she left the building and waved to security. Whether she wanted it to or not, her life was about to change radically. When she had phoned her father during her lunch break, he was overjoyed by the news. She smiled to herself; at least he'd be happy.

She dressed up for her last day at the design house. She wouldn't look out of place at OXO Tower Bar. For cocktails with a view, it was one of the best spots in London. Olivia Grey Designs had hosted several functions there.

Getting out of the elevator, her gaze drifted over to the expansive windows and she looked out over the river Thames at Saint Paul's Cathedral and the London skyline. Why did William insist on basing himself in Dublin instead of one of the financial capitals of the world? There were several things about him that surprised her.

***

He watched her look out at the view and not for him. Olivia had made a comment at dinner that Bridget would miss being in London and didn't seem overly keen to work in Ireland for a year.

He had discovered something else interesting about Ms. North. She was the daughter of one of the previous owners of the Donne Golf Club. Could this have been the reason she had disparaged his father? It didn't make sense. His father hadn't been involved in the purchase or restoration. He had been dead for more than five years when Thomas North, along with two partners, had attempted to resurrect the Donne. They had enough money to purchase it, but not to do any upgrades. It slowly sank into bankruptcy.

She scanned the bar looking for him, and when he caught her gaze, his body reacted. She wore a fitted sleeveless dress that gracefully hugged her feminine curves.

He stood and greeted her with a handshake. "Today was your last day at Olivia's design studio?" It didn't surprise him that Olivia had ushered her out the door. His sister wanted Breen saved.

Bridget nodded and slipped into the seat across from him and he signaled for the waiter to bring another glass.

"I've already selected a wine. Is that fine or would you care for something else?"

"It's fine." She hid her emotions well. Olivia had

told him that she'd cried over leaving. It made him rethink his plans. He didn't want an employee who had to be convinced to stick it out. He needed someone who wanted to be there.

The waiter placed a glass in front of her and poured the Cabernet Sauvignon.

Lifting his glass, he said, "To hard work and some pleasurable experiences over the next year."

She touched her glass to his and took a sip of the wine.

Sadness clung to her this evening and a stab of guilt pricked his emotions. Maybe he shouldn't have insisted on her involvement. "Olivia said that you decided to join my management team but I'd like to hear it from you. Are you excited?"

Bridget touched the stem of her wine glass. "I'm nervous. I hope it all goes well."

He took a sip of wine. "I've sent contracts over and have spoken to Patrick Breen a few times. The biggest obstacle we face is dragging them into the current century. I'll want you to work on expanding their marketing reach. I've hired an advertising firm in Dublin and will put them at your disposal."

Bridget glanced down at her hands. "I'll need a few days to sort out living arrangements."

"Doesn't your father live in Dublin?"

She looked at him. "Yes. But he has a studio flat so I couldn't possibly stay there."

"I live in a converted pub with ten bedrooms. You're welcome to stay there while you're looking for a place."

She shook her head. "I wouldn't want to trouble you."

"My housekeeper, Mrs. Blake, adores guests and I'm not returning for several days. There's a bike race here in the UK that I'm doing with my sister's husband, Alistair." Why did he feel the need to help her?

Bridget smoothed out the fabric of her dress. "Olivia mentioned that you own a cycling company."

It was the best investment he had made. "Yes, I've been pleased with the results. With a small investment, it has grown into a powerhouse in the industry."

She fidgeted with her pendant necklace. "What happens if Breen doesn't bring the same results?"

He considered whether she would bolt after a few weeks. Working on his management team took resourcefulness and the ability to deal with risk. "They don't require a ton of capital. Their issue, beyond needing to integrate technology, is that banks are not lending to companies in the garment industry. It's too risky."

She met his gaze. "But you're not afraid of risk?"

His mind was on other risks. "If you want to make money, then you need to be able to tolerate risk."

She took another swallow of wine. "Is money that important to you? Weren't you left a huge amount of it?"

He leaned closer to her and said in a low voice, "My financial portfolio is probably a topic that should be off limits."

She lifted her chin. "Why? Are you ashamed of how you make money?"

He shrugged. "No, Bridget. I'm ashamed of

nothing. Not the choices I've made or my family. But my financial worth is none of your business." Why did he let her get under his skin?

She glanced away. "I didn't mean to offend you. I'm just trying to understand what you hope to gain."

He poured them both more wine. "I'm hosting a dinner tomorrow night at my flat. I'm inviting several couples and I would like you to join us. The topic is going to be Breen, and I thought you could pick up a few samples from Olivia."

She sat back. "Are these investors?"

He didn't want a reluctant employee. "Yes. It occurred to me that instead of using my own capital on this purchase, I could bring in a silent investor. I'll choose one of three at the end of the evening. Your role will be to talk about the industry, the company, and the products."

Her eyes grew wider. "What if they ask something that I don't know?"

Something about the move troubled her. "Say that you'll have to find out and get back to them. They already have some of the business documents, so they know the basics."

She nodded and took a sip of her wine.

He needed her loyalty. "There's something else. You're expected to sign a non-disclosure agreement. You may speak with my sister about social issues or observations about the industry, but you may not relate any specific business knowledge or conversations."

She touched her collarbone. "Why?"

He met her gaze. "Because there's family and then there's business. I tell Olivia and Fionn a great deal, but it's my information to share."

Her voice rose. "What should I tell her if she asks? I signed an agreement not to answer her questions?"

"I adore my sister, but for the next year, your loyalty has to be with me. If she asks, tell her to speak with me directly."

After they finished their wine, William paid the bill and walked her to the elevator.

He pressed the button. "Should I arrange for a car service to take you home?"

She shook her head. "No. My aunt's flat is within walking distance. I'll see you tomorrow."

He checked his phone. "I'll text you the address for tomorrow night. It's a formal dinner."

Watching her leave, he realized he never asked her about her father. He had assumed that taking the position was a good deal for her, but something told him that the Donne Manor Hotel and Golf Resort was going to bring up baggage for her. It couldn't have been easy to watch her father slide into bankruptcy. It was odd—seeing Bridget again made him question whether she could handle the pressure of resurrecting failing companies. She seemed to hold some type of resentment but he couldn't decide if it was the golf course.

Chapter 5

William walked into the church the next morning and his heart softened. Both of his sisters were happily married and his nieces and small nephew held the promise of a better future for the Bolles family. He was lucky to be a part of all of this craziness. There was such love. It was also a paparazzi nightmare. Olivia and Fionn drew a ton of attention. Everyone, it seemed, wanted a photograph of their nephew in his custom baptismal gown.

The ceremony was precious and he held his three-year- old niece, Madeline, in his arms while Anna and Alistair took the baby up onto the altar with the godparents. William worried when his mother had complained bitterly about Anna using their father's name, but now that he had met his tiny nephew, he felt differently. It was a beautiful acknowledgement, but in the end the little boy would grow up to be his own person. His father would have been proud of his daughters and the life they had each created for themselves.

At the end of the ceremony, Gothic music rang out as the family allowed a few photographs before getting into a series of limousines. There was a private reception held back at Anna and Alistair's mansion outside of London.

Fionn approached him after the luncheon. "Let's take a drink outside."

William had enormous respect for Fionn. He had been part of his life for as long as he could remember. His father had stepped in when Fionn was a teenager and his father, an old friend of Oliver's, had taken his life. Fionn was considered brilliant with numbers and Oliver had taken him under his wing and eventually brought him into the business. When William was seventeen and his father died tragically, Fionn was there to pick up the pieces and make sure that he survived.

William poured Irish whiskey into two crystal glasses and handed one to Fionn.

Walking outside, they found a round table away from the festivities.

Fionn took a sip of whiskey. "Olivia convinced you to buy Breen."

He took in a deep breath. "I had doubts at first, but their product is excellent. They need a revamp of their marketing and Liv recommended Bridget North."

"Liv is going to miss her." After a brief pause, Fionn asked, "Is your golf resort continuing to bleed money?" There wasn't any judgment in Fionn's tone, but the question rattled him.

William glanced out at the back gardens. He didn't want to let on how desperate the situation had become. "It'll right itself. The place is magnificent. You should take a few days off and play eighteen with me."

He nodded. "Will, don't make the mistake of over-leveraging yourself. The entire thing could go south. If you need help, let me know."

Taking another swallow of whiskey, William said, "I'd come to you if the situation were dire, but it's going to work."

Fionn leaned closer. "What are you trying to prove? The cycling company was a good move. You had an interest and seem to enjoy the involvement, but the golf resort is complicated and my guess is it's putting pressure on your other companies. Now you've bought a failing hat company. I thought you had plans to join me in New York and London."

He ran a hand through his hair. "I'll eventually base myself in London and New York. But I'm determined to have my own company under the name Bolles."

Fionn shook his head. "It's not a smart move, Will. Your father is not remembered kindly. Finding a partner and using a different company name would only help you in the long run."

William took a sip of whiskey and then looked at Fionn. "I'm not afraid of using the Bolles name. It's my name. My legacy."

"He has been gone a long time." Fionn put a hand on his shoulder. "He'd have been proud of you."

Fionn's daughters, Beatrice and Addy, interrupted them and both men joined the larger family gathering in the dining room.

***

The next evening, Bridget walked into William's building and the doorman directed her upstairs to the twentieth floor. Her nerves were on hyper alert. She was moving to Dublin the next day, and having to help orchestrate a formal dinner for investors was too much. How could she possibly convince others that it was a smart move?

Knocking on the door to the flat, she waited for a servant to answer it. Instead, William opened the door himself, wearing a formal suit, and her heart accelerated. She had chosen a gown in a light gray that was short yet elegant.

He stepped back. "Come in. You're punctual."

Was he trying to remind her of her position as an employee? "Yes. In most situations, it seems to be a good idea."

His eyes raked over her and he stepped closer. "You look beautiful. Navigating the chemistry between us will be a challenge."

Bridget crossed her arms. "Maybe you shouldn't have put us in that position."

He smiled briefly and his eyes held a challenge. "Maybe not. The chef and his server are in the kitchen preparing the meal. I'm getting the drinks ready. Would you care for one?"

She walked into the living room. "I'd better not. It wouldn't be great to get tipsy and embarrass you on my first day."

He followed her into the room. "Relax. You'll enjoy the guests and I doubt any serious discussion of money will take place. It's more about providing a set time to discuss the potential and get them excited about the big picture."

Bridget wandered over to the display that had been set up of various hats that she had dropped off earlier. "Did you want me to model any of these?" She picked up a gray silk hat with netting and placed it on her head.

"I might enjoy it more if it were lingerie."

She placed the hat back among the displayed items. He was playful and friendly at times and then would shift so it was impossible to read him. He couldn't possibly intend to encourage her attraction to him. It would make their business relationship awkward and tension-filled. It was a mistake she had never made, getting involved with someone at the office.

"What can I do to help?"

William continued to arrange the bottles of seltzer and alcohol. "Can you check the table settings?"

Bridget walked into the expansive dining area with a view of Hyde Park and beyond. The table was set formally with white and gold china and a floral centerpiece.

William intrigued her. Not many single men would host an elaborate dinner. Most would book a private dining room in an exclusive restaurant. She continued on to the kitchen and said hello to the chef and his assistant. They were polite but busy, so she wandered back to the living room.

"The table is perfect. Can I change my mind and have a glass of red wine?"

Pouring two glasses, he handed her one. "It's a French Merlot that should pair well with the appetizer."

***

William sat on one of the grey modern sofas flanking the fireplace. "The couples coming tonight have invested with me in the past. For a time, I was interested in mining, and two of them invested in an Argentine mine; the other was an investor in a sports apparel company. Each investment did well."

Bridget stood by the large windows overlooking the city. "Do you usually have a formal dinner when you're looking for investors?"

Watching her graceful profile against the windows, he wondered how she had become interested in high fashion. "This is the first time. Typically, I'd create a short list and schedule private meetings. But Breen is an easy investment and will have wide appeal."

Turning, she faced him. "You almost turned down Breen. I had the impression that you were doing a favor for Olivia but weren't keen on getting involved."

The timing had not been ideal. "My energy and resources are focused elsewhere. But in the end, it's a solid investment and not difficult to find silent partners."

"Olivia told me that you've taken on a challenging venture and that problems don't unnerve you."

He watched her quietly for a moment before taking a sip of his wine. "I won't worry you with the issues before this dinner. Better that you're fresh and positive."

Bridget moved closer and sat down on a nearby upholstered chair. "I'd rather understand the problems facing your company."

He crossed his legs and stretched out. "It's basically strategy and planning. After you've settled in Dublin, I'll pull together the management team and you can meet everyone. You'll be the youngest, and the only woman. The four others are all men I met while cycling. I formed a management company seven years ago, Maglia Rosa Investments, creating a way to work with a team to revamp companies."

Taking a sip of wine, Bridget asked, "So not being a rider, I'm probably at a disadvantage?"

He smiled. "You could always take up the sport." He'd love to see her out on a bicycle.

She gazed at him. "What does Maglia Rosa mean? The pink shirt?"

Her brown eyes reminded him of dark honey. "It's a cycling term. It's used to refer to the race leader. I've seen other colors used as well. The concept was that we'd invest in projects that we could get to market before anyone else. It's worked well, but the team needs to expand."

Bridget reached forward and placed her glass down. "Who is part of the team currently?"

He could barely take his eyes off of her. "I'll be easier when you actually meet them. Alex—he's known for his analytical insights and calm, logical thinking. Jeremy, the accountant on the team, is careful with money and keeps an eye on cash flow and expenses." He smiled at her and watched as she tried to process the details. "Merle has a background in launching start-ups. He likes new challenges and is about to become a father. The last member, Arlo, has a background in mechanical engineering and likes adventure. He's riding in a bike race in northern Spain at the moment."

The doorbell rang and he rose to greet his guests. Within a short time, everyone arrived and there was excitement and good-natured joking.

***

Bridget relaxed and enjoyed the evening. The women were interested in the hats and it took only a small amount of effort for them to try on the samples. One of the younger couples, Francesca and Alberto, started the bidding over dinner.

At one point William said, "It's not my intention to have a bidding war. I wanted you all to have the opportunity to get involved. We've worked well in the past."

Alberto said, "Create a funding agreement and we all can contribute a million pounds." It was an arrangement agreed to among everyone at the table and the conversation shifted to politics and then the economy.

After the last couple left, Bridget said, "You made that look rather easy."

William removed his tie and undid the top button of his shirt. "If you bring together the right people and have a solid approach or offering, then it merely requires having the patience to let it happen."

Retrieving the small handbag she came with from a side table, she said, "I should go. Thank you for this evening."

He led her to the door. "It's grown late. I'll walk with you."

She stood facing him and shook her head. "I can get a taxi."

He picked up his keys off of a table in the foyer and opened the door. "It's a perfect evening to enjoy the night."

They walked along the sidewalk together, and he slowed his pace to match hers. He spoke about plans for Breen and she realized that he was planning a year out. She had only considered the employees' expected response to the change of ownership. She had been busy finishing her work for Olivia.

They passed by a popular nightclub and William easily deflected a man who nearly collided into her.

She stepped back. "Your reflexes are speedy."

He took her hand and they crossed the street. "There's a path through the park. It may be easier then dealing with the crowded street."

He released her hand when they stepped through the park gate, and he led her to a grass-covered field.

The heels she had worn were more for fashion than covering slippery terrain. "I didn't realize we would be walking on grass or I may have chosen other shoes."

He slowed and looked at her feet. "Sorry. I should have realized. Do you want to walk barefoot?"

"Maybe. I need to find a place to sit for a moment." Looking around, she noticed a small stone bench near a monument, but it was a few hundred feet away.

William picked her up and she stilled. "I'm sure I can walk."

He smiled at her, but his expression was difficult to read in the darkness. "At least you won't twist your ankle."

Her breathing became rushed and she tried to calm her nerves. Her body was reacting to him and her reaction was wild and erratic. It crossed all sorts of lines for him to physically carry her. He was now her boss and she needed some distance.

***

He shouldn't play with fire, but she was

impossibly tempting. Her proper attitude and reluctant manner made him want to melt away all of her erected barriers. But it wouldn't serve him. He wanted her for her marketing mind and rapport with employees, not for himself. Her sharp tongue had already torn the flesh from his bones. He didn't need a repeat.

He placed her on the stone bench and watched in fascination as she removed a shoe and then unrolled a silk stocking.

Bridget didn't look up. "Would you mind giving me a moment?"

Her seductive movements held his attention. She reached under her dress and undid the other stocking, rolling it down and then taking off her shoe. She put the stockings in her small handbag and then picked up her shoes.

His heartbeat pounded relentlessly. "I'd have guessed that you would wear um... pantyhose."

She smiled. "It'd be odd to work in fashion and wear pantyhose."

He had made a calculated mistake thinking he could spend time with the beautiful and captivating marketing executive and not fall under her spell. But he wanted more from her than a night in bed. She'd help him figure out what to do with the golf resort that was bleeding him dry.

"Besides, stockings are far more comfortable."

He wanted to explore her body but refused to act on the desire. The darkness hid the evidence of his need and somehow made their interaction seem dreamlike, as if they were moving in slow motion.

"I wouldn't know."

He stepped closer to her and watched as her eyes

met his. He couldn't see her pupils, only the deep brown of her gaze. One kiss. He would kiss her briefly and be satisfied with one taste. Reaching forward, he touched the side of her face and gently traced her cheekbone with the tip of his thumb. He could feel his body heating. How could she turn him on with barely a touch?

He stopped himself. The way desire surged through his veins, a kiss wouldn't satisfy him. Bridget touched his arm and moved the smallest fraction closer to him. He looked down into her gaze and tried to interpret her thoughts.

Why was he denying himself? They were adults and could move past one brief encounter. He brought his other hand up and cupped her face. She drew in a breath and he covered her lips with his.

He lightly kissed her twice, barely touching her, and held himself in check, ready to stop, when she said, "Kiss me properly."

After a fraction of a second, he pulled her closer and deepened the kiss. She opened her mouth fully under his and he increased the pressure wanting to devour her. He took could feel her tongue duel with his. His hands moved to the back of her head to hold her steady under his exploration, and his fingers touched her silky hair.

She ran her hands over his pressed shirt and he wanted to feel them on his bare skin, but resisted unbuttoning it for her. Instead, he gathered her more fully against him and her breasts pushed against his chest as he continued to explore her mouth. His own breathing sounded hurried and he pressed a kiss into her neck to allow them a moment to regain some sanity.

It was foolish; he wanted to claim her as his. She brought out a possessive streak in him that made him feel like a cave dweller. He needed to regain some semblance of sanity.

***

Bridget pulled in an uneven breath. William Bolles made her want more things she shouldn't. He was the enemy, and yet she couldn't get enough of him. She wanted to strip his shirt off and feel the muscles in his chest.

She pressed her lips to his again. He deepened the kiss and she could feel an intense heat build within her. He moved his hands over her bottom and drew her closer to him. She wanted more from him. Her hand slipped down and traced the shape of his hard length. He drew in a shuddering breath and pulled her closer, then pushed her away.

A daze covered her brain and it took a second for her to realize that he wanted to end their seductive encounter.

"I lost my head. I'm sorry. I shouldn't have allowed this to happen."

He regretted kissing her. If she were being honest with herself, she should regret it. They were about to spend a year working together. But it had felt incredible and had allowed her to lose herself completely. It never happened that way for her. Typically if a man kissed her at the end of a date, her mind would wander to mundane tasks. She never lost her head. But why him? Why did it have to be William Bolles?

"It was a mistake." She touched her tongue to her

lips and turned away from him.

Glancing out at the deserted park, she thought that it had been a fantastic experience. One she had wanted to continue. But then the practical side of her intervened and she realized who she was dealing with. He had too much entitlement and power in his hands. His father had been irresponsible and had started her father's downfall with a throwaway comment.

"Can you walk?"

She nodded and followed him over the expansive lawn. The cool grass grounded her, taking her mind off of their shared encounter. She couldn't quite remember why he had kissed her or why she had asked him to kiss her properly. It was almost as if it were a dream, and she would wake up any moment.

She stopped when they reached the sidewalk and reached down to put on her shoes. It was odd to feel so self-conscious. Normally, she didn't let down her guard and never acted on impulse.

Standing up straight, she said, "It's only another two blocks. I'm fine on my own."

William ran a hand through his short hair. "We need to talk about what happened in the park."

She looked away from him. "No. We should put it down to a moment of madness and forget it."

He lightly touched her lower back. "Nothing is that easy."

Crossing her arms, she said, "This will be."

They continued walking in silence until they reached her aunt's building. "I don't think it's a good idea for you to come in."

He smiled at her. "I'll see you in Dublin in a week."

"Cheers, William." Bridget pushed through the circular doors and didn't allow herself to glance back at him.

Why did he kiss her? It complicated everything. Relocating to Dublin would be tough enough without adding another layer of social pressure. Instead of being wildly attracted to him, she should be erecting tougher barriers. He was a Bolles and born into a type of privilege that she would never understand.

Chapter 6

The next day, Bridget threw the covers off of her and got out of bed before the sun rose. Stretching her arms overhead, she glanced at her large suitcase packed and ready to go. Her flight from Heathrow to Dublin was in less than three hours. Leaving behind her sensibly ordered life in London filled her with anxiety.

Walking into the kitchen, she turned the kettle on and then checked her travel documents. She poured boiling water into a small teapot and then headed to the hall bathroom. Pushing aside the curtain, she turned on the water and went through her morning routine.

Nearly twenty minutes later, she walked back into the small kitchen wearing a white linen belted dress with black sandals. Pouring herself a cup of tea, she moved into the sitting area and tried to decide if she had forgotten anything important. Her Aunt Cora had insisted that she could ship whatever she needed, but she wanted to bring anything essential. Checking her handbag again, she gathered her suitcase, laptop bag, and a water bottle.

When her short flight landed in Dublin, she made her way to baggage claim. She took in the sights and sounds of the familiar airport. Clutching her arms to her chest, she reminded herself that her new position was a promotion. So why did she keep imagining ways to escape?

Her phone rang with an unknown number and she answered it.

"Hello."

"Hi, Bridget. This is Mary Blake, William's housekeeper. He gave me your number."

Bridget reached forward and pulled her heavy suitcase from the conveyer belt. "Hi, Mary. I've just arrived in Dublin."

"Shall I come and fetch you from the airport?"

She smiled. "It's not necessary. I can get a taxi."

"Okay, dear. I have everything ready for your stay."

Bridget scanned the baggage area for the exit. "I don't want to trouble you."

"It's no trouble. See you in a little while."

Dropping her phone back into her bag, Bridget groaned to herself. She had planned to find a reasonably priced hotel, but now she found herself heading to William's residence. It crossed all sorts of professional lines to stay at his house, even if he wasn't there.

Standing in line for the next taxi, she kept a tight hold on her bags. When it was her turn, the driver put her suitcase in the trunk and she climbed into the back of the vehicle.

She gave the address to the driver and then leaned back against the leather seat. With any luck she would find a furnished flat within a day or two. She had scheduled several appointments for later that day and the next.

The taxi driver brought her to a quaint brick-paved street a short distance from the center of Dublin. The old stone pub had a wrought-iron fence and a short path leading to the front door.

Stepping out onto the sidewalk, she paid the driver and took her suitcase from him, repositioning her other bags.

Dragging her suitcase up the short path, Bridget turned the ornate doorbell and stepped back.

Mary pulled the door open and gestured for her to come in. "Welcome, dear. It's a pleasure to have you stay here."

Bridget smiled and stepped inside the stone residence. The wooden floors shone brilliantly and a soft light filtered in from the expansive formal living room.

Readjusting her handbag, she told the housekeeper, "I expected to find a hotel. I hope it isn't any trouble having me here."

Mary clutched her chest. "Oh, heavens, no. I was delighted when William called."

William's flat in London reminded her of luxury and opulence, but this place seemed understated. It reminded her of old Dublin. Mary was dressed casually, wearing old jeans with a floral t-shirt.

"Thank you. It's nice not to stay in a hotel."

Mary took her suitcase and said, "I'll show you to a spare room and then I can make some tea."

After placing her belongings in the spacious guest room that overlooked the back garden, Bridget followed the housekeeper to the kitchen.

There was a large island with a marble

countertop. An assortment of vegetables had been chopped and were placed on a cutting board.

Mary removed the cover to a large pot simmering on the stove and stirred the contents with a wooden spoon. "I'm making a lamb stew for dinner."

"It smells delicious."

The housekeeper moved around the kitchen, putting on the kettle and taking out a few items from the refrigerator.

Bridget took her handbag over to the table and retrieved her phone. "I have a meeting with a real estate broker this afternoon to see a few furnished flats."

"Flats in Dublin can be difficult to find."

She glanced down at her phone. "I'm not going to be nit-picky. If the broker can find something available and furnished, I'll probably take it."

Mary served her tea and a selection of small sandwiches and dried fruit. "You'd do better being fussy. You may live there for a long time."

"I'm going to be working quite a bit and possibly travelling, so I don't think it matters much."

Placing a dish towel on her shoulder, Mary went over to stir the stew. "Do you have a pet or children?"

Bridget laughed, despite her efforts to hold it in. "No. I don't have children or any pets."

Mary let out a heavy sigh. "So, you work all of the time and don't have any responsibilities?"

Taking a sip of tea, she considered the question. Her father was her responsibility, but she didn't want to reveal too much about herself. "I grew up in Dublin and my father lives here. Moving back from London will give me a chance to spend more time with him."

She used her phone to check her bank balance again. It was unbelievable that she had enough money in her account to buy him a small cottage outside of the city.

"That's lovely, dear. He must be overjoyed."

Bridget nodded. "Yes. He's happy that I've come back to Dublin for a year." Checking the time, she stood up. "I'm going to pop out for a bit to check on a few flats. I'll see you in a few hours."

"No need to rush. The stew will be ready whenever you get back."

"See you later." Bridget gathered her phone and handbag and left the house.

***

Nearly two hours later, she stood in the center of a furnished flat, and turning to the broker, said, "I'm ready to sign a lease."

The broker, a woman in her late fifties with gray hair and old-fashioned glasses, frowned and said, "Um, you haven't seen many places yet. I have a whole list to show you."

Bridget smiled. "I appreciate your thoroughness, but this flat is fine."

The broker gave her a blank look. "You haven't even told me what you're looking for beyond needing a place right away and that it should be furnished."

Nodding, Bridget moved towards the door. "I've just accepted a position at The Breen Hat Company and want to start straightaway."

The woman adjusted her glasses. "If you're sure, but it wouldn't be difficult to show you more places."

"I'm sure." She needed to sort out something for her father and she didn't want to spend too much time at William's house.

The broker opened the door and stepped out into the hallway of the building. "Let's go back to my office and we can make the arrangements."

Bridget walked down the staircase and looked at the architectural detail of the building. "How old is this building?"

Pulling out a piece of paper, the broker said, "The listing shows 1948 with a renovation about fifteen years ago. The flat is small, but you'll be able to walk to South Great Georges Street, Grafton Street, and all of the landmarks. There are many pubs and restaurants nearby."

"The location works well and the flat has some character."

The broker smiled. "It's true."

Bridget left the broker's office with a signed lease agreement and a move-in date for that Saturday. Before returning to William's house, she stopped in a little shop and picked up box of handmade chocolates for Mary Blake.

    ***

The next day, after visiting The Breen Hat Company in the morning, Bridget took the bus to her father's neighborhood in Dublin.

Getting off by his rented flat, she scanned the sidewalk for her father and smiled when she spotted him feeding the birds. Only the tourists fed the birds, but Thomas North believed in living in the moment. He looked thinner these days, but in general had fared well. Other men would have allowed bankruptcy to defeat them, but he kept a positive attitude.

"Hello, Tom." It rattled her nerves occasionally

that she addressed her father by his given name, but he never objected. She guessed it was part of her taking care of him and it relieved him of some of the responsibility of being a father.

"Bridget, you look so pretty today, dear."

She kissed his cheek. "The estate broker is waiting for us at the pub." She had spent the last couple of days arguing with him about purchasing a small cottage. She had finally prevailed. She needed the win. She had given up her life in London for the next year on the whim of Olivia and William. At least she would secure a permanent home for her father. It would keep her motivated and working hard for the next twelve months. It would mean she wouldn't have to worry about her father or struggle as much. Maybe when she returned to London, she would be able to rent her own flat.

Thomas put his cap on. "I spoke with him this morning and asked for him to look for cottages over by the Donne Golf Resort. It would be a good investment with the course opening in the next year. The value will skyrocket."

"Tom, that golf resort has gone through many owners. As we know firsthand, it's a money pit. Won't it depress you to see it each day?"

"On the contrary, I plan to play golf there one day."

She bit her lip. There was no point dragging up the past.

The estate broker was a laid-back and easy young fellow who spent considerable time taking them around. Tom chose a small cottage that needed a little work, and she signed an offer. She hoped he could move in within the month and then begin to see a different future for himself.

    ***

William flew his aircraft into the private airstrip outside of Dublin. He had spent the last week trying to banish Bridget from his mind with an intense and grueling bike race, but with little result. How could she so easily capture his interest? He had plenty of women throwing themselves at him. Why did she rattle him so easily?

Maybe he should send her back to Olivia. But he had no desire to speak with his sister about the issue. What would he possibly say? She gets under my skin and I don't want her around? He refused to admit a weakness. He would deal with his attraction to her in some way or another. And if Olivia had any suspicion that he found Bridget desirable, she would gently encourage it.

Frustration coursed through his veins. He called his assistant and had him set up an early morning meeting for his executive team, instructing him to invite Bridget.

Walking into his house, he called out to Mary.

She came out of the kitchen wiping her hands on her apron. "Ah, you've returned in one piece this time."

"Is Bridget here?"

"No. She stayed three nights and then moved to a flat near the Loft Market."

Why did that irritate him? She should focus on her career. He didn't need her underfoot.

His housekeeper smiled at him. "Can I get you a light meal?"

"No," he said in irritation.

Watching her retreat back to the kitchen, he ran a hand through his hair. He could swear that he could smell Bridget's perfume; he had to be hallucinating.

Walking into the kitchen, he said, "I apologize if I seem irritated. It has nothing to do with you."

She continued chopping an onion. "It's fine. I'm putting the finishing sauce together for a seafood chowder and thought maybe you'd ask Bridget to join you for dinner. She had asked several times when you would return."

"Bridget North is a new employee that I brought in to help The Breen Hat Company. Olivia had recommended her." Why was he explaining himself?

"Are you going to ask her to dinner?"

"I doubt it." He headed to his office on the other side of the converted pub. He needed to immerse himself in work.

***

An hour later, William threw down his pen. He needed to escape his office. Stripping off his jeans and shirt, he put on biking shorts and a shirt. He left the house and rode his favorite route through the city. He was hard-wired to push himself physically. It was late afternoon and the sun was oppressive, but he welcomed the intensity.

Coming back to his neighborhood drenched in sweat, he slowed his pace. Deciding to invite Bridget for dinner, he unclipped his feet and got off his bike.

Avoiding her was a bad move; it fueled his erotic thoughts. His body remembered each sensation and touch when he had kissed her in the park. Their interactions needed to get back to a professional association. The golf course required his full focus and Bridget would need to delve into the issues at Breen.

William opened the ornate iron gate that protected his property and walked his bike down the side driveway. Stepping into the garage, he lifted his bicycle and hung it on steel hooks.

Taking the covered passageway into the house, he called out, "Mary?"

Coming out of the kitchen, his housekeeper waited patiently for him.

"Could you call Bridget and ask if she could come over for dinner? I'm going to take a shower."

Nodding, Mary went back towards the kitchen.

***

Bridget disconnected the call and threw her phone onto the sofa. Instead of unpacking tonight, she was expected to entertain William Bolles. She hoped he didn't want an update on Breen. She had spent the last week sorting out a place to live and helping her father.

After taking a quick shower, she chose an ivory-and-black tweed dress from her closet. Holding up the dress, she noted that the contrasting geometric-patterned straight skirt looked professional and serious. She needed to move their association back into a strictly business realm. The sooner she got The Breen Hat Company back to being profitable, the sooner she could resume her life in London.

Deciding to walk the dozen or so blocks over to William's house, Bridget thought about the challenges facing the hat company. The employees were hard-working and earnest, but their methods and processes were firmly cemented in the past.

She stopped at a flower cart and asked for a

bouquet of white lilies. The older gentleman assembling the flowers winked at her. Handing him twenty euro, she took the wrapped flowers and continued on her route.

As she reached William's house, Bridget stood on the sidewalk looking at the converted stone pub for a minute. She had so many memories from her childhood of her mother sending her down to the pub to bring her father back. He could always be found in the center of a gathering, talking about one scheme or another. It rarely occurred to him to just come home for dinner.

She walked up the front pathway and turned the old-fashioned door chime. It made sense that William lived in a converted pub in some ways, but it also made her curious. Most of the super wealthy lived outside of the city limits in mansions. Why would he choose a converted pub?

Mary answered the door and invited her in.

"You look lovely, dear. William should be down shortly. Would you like to wait on the terrace or in the living room?"

Bridget handed her the lilies. "These are for you."

Mary smiled and scrunched up her face. "You didn't have to bring me anything."

"I saw these and thought of you." Bridget smelled the sweet fragrance. "I'll wait on the terrace."

Stepping outside, Bridget placed her handbag on a side wood table and walked over to the low stone wall that separated the patio from an expansive lawn and garden area. A high privacy fence at the back protected the outside space from the city.

When she heard the door open, she turned and

locked glances with William. His hair looked wet from a shower and he wore jeans with a fitted charcoal t-shirt showing a cycling logo.

He stepped forward and kissed her lightly on the cheek. Her stomach muscles clenched. She didn't want to feel drawn to him.

Keeping her voice neutral, she said, "I hope you enjoyed the race."

He stepped back from her. His sculpted body showed off how much time he spent cycling. "Alistair is a tremendous competitor, so it was extreme in a good way."

She pushed her hair behind her shoulder and thought about what to bring up. "Do you compete often?"

"It depends. Would you like ale or wine this evening?"

She surprised herself by saying, "Ale." In London, she drank only wine or champagne, but being back in Dublin made her nostalgic.

He returned with two glass bottles of McSorley's Irish Pale Ale and opened them on a built-in opener by the door before handing her the cold bottle. "There are some advantages to owning an old pub."

She smiled. "What made you purchase this place?"

He sat down on one of the wooden chairs with cushions and gestured for her to join him. "The stone building was collapsing and I was looking for a project a few years ago."

Bridget sank into the chair next to him. He was driven and obviously successful, but he also seemed to spend much of his time alone. "Are you happy being in the city center? Often entrepreneurs with a hectic work life chose somewhere quiet and remote."

William took a swallow of his ale. "At first, it was just me and I could walk for a meal or takeout. I like being close to everything, but inside the old stone building, there's history and as much solitude as any man would want."

She took a sip of the cold ale. "So you found Mrs. Blake to help you?"

William stretched out his legs. "She found me. She had worked in the pub for years, and so when she saw me working on the gardens in the front, she stopped and gently suggested I needed a cook and housekeeper."

"So you hired her?"

He nodded. "I needed someone to keep me on a straight and narrow path. I'd often skip meals and work for days on end."

Bridget looked out at the gardens. "This place was probably popular. It must have had a long history of locals stopping in for a drink after work." Her father spent too much time in pubs. It was part of the culture in Dublin, but it didn't work for everyone.

William sat forward and took another swallow from his bottle. "Maybe even some drunken brawls. A pub is also a place where milestones are celebrated and strong social bonds formed."

***

She wore a conservative dress probably to remind both of them that they had a professional connection but he could only concentrate on the way it wrapped around flat stomach and the curve of her feminine hips. "I'm assuming that you've been settling in and haven't had a chance to get over to Breen yet?"

She nodded slowly. "I've been helping my father with a few things now that I'm living in Dublin. I also thought it would be a good idea to get some direction from your executive team before I throw myself into Breen. I'm not clear on the overarching changes that you plan to implement."

He placed his empty bottle on a nearby table. "I've heard of your father in connection to the golf course."

She looked away. "Thomas North is a rather common name in Ireland."

It had to be her father. It was an odd coincidence that Bridget had been hired by Olivia while her father had been a previous owner of the golf course he eventually purchased.

He didn't believe in coincidences, but after a ton of digging, he hadn't found any connection between his father and Thomas North. He had even looked into the background of her aunt who lived in London. She had been a buyer in the fashion industry for years and probably mentioned Olivia to Bridget, but it didn't explain why Thomas North would put his last euro into the golf course. Or why Bridget had a deep resentment for his father.

"The first night we met, you had said my father had given shoddy investment advice. Did he recommend that your father invest in a golf course not that far from here?"

From the paleness of her skin, he knew that there was a connection.

"My investment group purchased the course two years ago and I'm curious about why your father would have decided to invest."

He watched her get up and move away from the table. She looked out over the back garden and kept her back towards him. "It was a foolish investment on his part and he lost everything."

Why did the conversation make her so uncomfortable? "A golf resort is not an easy investment. One would need huge reserves to resurrect it. But your father must have had a local connection that he thought might help with the project."

She turned back to face him. "No. He was merely foolish and a dreamer. He had no larger plan."

He crossed his arms. "I find that hard to believe. He must have had ideas, a plan. I'd like to speak with him about it."

She shook her head. "No. It would only encourage his fantasies."

He sat forward. "Bridget, I need local expertise. There is a dark shadow hanging over the course and locals don't want to be involved. Your father may have a few ideas."

Bridget clutched the pendant necklace she wore. "You requested my involvement in Breen, not the golf course."

William stood up. "In trade for my purchase of Breen, Olivia signed over your employment contract for a year. The new contract doesn't specify Breen. It's understood that my employees will work on any of the companies that I acquire."

***

Her heart squeezed painfully. She couldn't bring herself to work on the golf course. She would have to find a way out. It had destroyed her family and nearly cost her father his life. The depression that had plagued him since the bankruptcy worried her each day. With her mother gone, he no longer had a reason to get up each morning. "I'm not going near the golf course. I'm not helping with marketing for it and I'm certainly not going to set up a meeting with my father."

Mary popped her head out of the door. "Would you like dinner on the terrace or in the dining room?"

"I'm not staying after all."

William turned towards his housekeeper. "Mary, the dining room is fine, and Ms. North will be staying, I believe, after we resolve something."

She watched the housekeeper disappear. The entire situation was awkward. She hated to inconvenience Mary, but there was no way she would be able to stomach any meal.

William faced her and lifted his hands palms up. "Why are you so upset?"

Bridget took in a calming breath. She needed to regain control. It would not be wise to show William how much this bothered her. "I've been gearing up for working at the hat company. I know nothing about running or renovating a golf course." She stepped further away from him. "My father was devastated by the bankruptcy and then soon after by my mother's death. To bring all of that up again won't do anyone any good."

"It might help him put it in perspective. He didn't have the resources to properly make a go of it. Now if there is a way to bring him in, it could be positive."

Bridget turned and faced him. "He doesn't hold any secrets about the place. He won't be able to help you."

He shrugged his shoulders. "Maybe not but it can't hurt to have a conversation."

Her arms were shaky. "Could I have a glass of water?"

William nodded and left the terrace. Why hadn't Olivia mentioned the golf course? Her mind raced back through various conversations. They had spoken about his obsession with cycling and flying his own airplane but not about the golf course. Maybe Olivia didn't think it was important.

He came back with a tall glass of water and pressed it into her hand. "Are you feeling all right?"

She took a sip of water. "I don't want to involve my father."

He pressed his lips together before saying, "You've little choice, Bridget. If you default on your contract, then you'll be required to repay the advance. An advance that you have already spent on a cottage for your father."

She gasped. "How could you possibly know that?"

He ran a hand through his hair. "I make it my business to understand my executives' financial circumstances. I need to know what your motivations are and why you may advocate for a particular decision or investment."

Her mind went blank. "That has to be an invasion of privacy. I have a right to confidentiality and not have every detail told to you."

"You signed the contract and agreed to divulge any expenditure over 5,000 euro."

How could she have signed the paperwork

without asking more questions? "Not on a personal basis. I agreed on disclosing business expenses."

He shrugged. "The contract specified personal financial transactions. Each executive owns shares in many companies, but for purposes of conflict of interest, I have to know about the financial connections and overlaps. I rely heavily on their advice. I need to know where their interests lie."

Her hands clenched into fists. "I can't imagine knowing that I purchased a cottage for my father would help further your business interests."

He shrugged. "It tells me that you're all in. You're not holding back, waiting to see if this experiment will work. Like it or not, you're committed for the next year."

Bridget met his gaze. "I fully intend to work at Breen and do everything within my power to make the company profitable. But I can't possibly help with the golf resort or involve my father."

His blue eyes deepened in intensity. "The executive meeting tomorrow morning is at the golf resort. It's the focus of my executive team. Breen is a tangent. I've given them the money to continue for the next several months so we have some time. The resort, on the other hand, is at a crucial stage."

She stood up straighter. "You brought me in knowing who my father was?"

William ran a hand through his hair. "No. It was a welcome coincidence. But you're seen as a marketing genius and I intended to get your help with the resort in addition to Breen. But now knowing that you could sway the locals, or your father could, I'm keen to make use of that connection."

Panic wound its way through her body. She couldn't allow him to systematically ruin everything she had built for herself. Going back would do that. It would bring up old resentments and paralyze her, preventing her from telling the truth. In this case, the truth was too painful. "I can't do it, William. The resort holds so many negative memories for me. I wouldn't be able to help, even if I wanted to."

He met her gaze and his focus didn't waver. "You'll have to get over the past. You have the skills and expertise to move the project forward, and I expect your full involvement."

Her body tightened. Involvement in the resort would in some ways tarnish the memories she had of her mother. She had promised her that she would move on and create a life for herself away from all the craziness.

His voice softened. "What are you so afraid of?"

She refused to give him insight into her fears. He would never understand. He grew up in a life of privilege and excess, not scraping by with barely enough to eat while listening to far-fetched schemes.

Her voice sounded fragile and unsure. "I'll speak with my father, but I doubt you'll get the outcome that you are expecting."

He held his hand up towards the house. "Let's go in for dinner. Mary makes an amazing fish chowder."

How was she going to survive this? William would have her father hanging on his every word and looking for encouragement. If she wasn't careful, her father would volunteer to spend his entire day helping out.

Or would it totally destroy him to see someone

else succeed where he failed?

Bridget wasn't sure, but either way, nothing could change the past.

Chapter 7

The next morning, Bridget waited for William outside her flat while professionals rushed to their destinations and school children strolled by in small groups. She had chosen her furnished flat based on the closeness to The Breen Hat Company. She hadn't considered that she would need to purchase a car, as the Donne Manor Hotel and Golf Resort was completely inaccessible by public transportation.

She called her father last night, and he seemed overjoyed that her new boss was the owner of the golf resort. They agreed to meet for coffee later in the morning. How would she keep a reasonable distance between William and her father? She wanted her work life to be separate from her personal life.

Rehearsing in her mind the questions she would ask, she tried to focus on the meeting ahead. She understood the fashion world. Marketing was focused on the consumer, and she had no knowledge of the hospitality industry or golf venues. How could she possibly be helpful?

She was probably overdressed. She wore a black Burberry skirt with a fitted white pressed shirt and slip-on Italian wedge heels. She had packed her luggage with fashion pieces meticulously collected from all of the sample sales she had frequented. She'd expected to be at Breen.

William double-parked his Land Rover and got out to open the door for her. He looked incredible in dark jeans and a bright orange racing jersey. His hair was neatly gelled and he wore reflective sunglasses.

"Ready to meet the team and see the golf resort?"

She climbed in and he shut the door.

He maneuvered back into traffic and she said, "This is not about me facing the past. I was never an owner of The Donne. But given everything I know about the resort, I highly doubt you'll turn it around."

He shifted gears. "Ah. You've so little faith. The hotel needs to be upgraded, but I've hired a gifted landscape architect and the course has been reimagined."

She looked out her window. "Have you been able to list the course in any of the major golf events?"

"The work has to be finished before it can qualify. This is why I need a local person to help with the negotiations."

The locals would not help him. It seems everyone had lost money in the local community trying to resurrect The Donne. It would be a public relations nightmare. "From everything I remember, the terrain was rocky and treacherous. I don't know how you'll manage to make it work."

He kept his eyes on the road. "The course has to be challenging, or it won't inspire top players to come."

She looked at his fierce profile. "I doubt the run-down hotel will inspire those top players to stay."

"You'd be surprised. With the right course, they

would probably stay in a tent. That was the mistake your father made—trying to upgrade the facilities first and then allowing those who do shoddy work to have control."

She crossed her arms. "If he made so many mistakes, why do you insist on meeting with him?"

He stopped at a red light. "Your father may have a connection to the local contractors. We need someone who can negotiate for us."

She placed a hand on her stomach. "He's a dreamer, not a hard-nosed negotiator."

"Without a dreamer, it would be hard to complete the project. Someone had to see the good in it. I played the course many times as a teenager, and it, for the lack of a better word, was magical. The way it drops off and you can see the ocean from every part of the course."

She looked at him, trying to take in his thought process. Discussing the course, he was about more than merely profit and loss. He had some sort of sentimental connection with the land. Like her father.

"Does your management team agree with seeking out Tom?"

He kept his gaze on the road. "They're perplexed at the moment. The Donne is hemorrhaging money. We've never taken on a long-term company or project that had this much risk. They need to dig in and find talent and expertise that they didn't know existed within themselves to make this work."

He'd be a tough boss. "Maybe you're asking too much of them?"

He glanced at her briefly. "They're well-compensated to succeed where others have failed.

We've turned around several companies that are now doing unimaginable sales. I know this will happen for The Donne."

He turned down the private road towards the golf course. Her heart squeezed painfully. The sweeping lawns were dramatic and she could see work happening in the distance.

She held her arms tightly around her body. "It's changed considerably, but I don't share your enthusiasm. You probably shouldn't bring me in, because I'm not able to be a cheerleader. I don't see success as a likely outcome."

"If you approach this with an open mind and give it a chance, then tell me you can't help, you can focus exclusively on Breen."

She turned towards him. "William, I belong at Breen. I have experience in the fashion industry, not within the hospitality arena."

Her words were met with silence and she began to feel uneasy. He had just asked her to withhold judgment and have an open mind. Surely she was capable of that? Even if this horrible place brought back terrible memories for her. Her father had spent the last few years of her mother's life throwing himself into this place and it was all for nothing.

***

William parked his vehicle near the conference center. Getting out, he breathed in the fresh scent of grass being cut. He waited for Bridget to climb out of the Range Rover and walk towards him. He found her fascinating. She had a high-fashion look, yet she seemed so grounded. Her negative thoughts about The Donne made him uneasy. Fionn had visited a few months back and had counseled him to give up and pull out of the project. The course might be a beast, but he wanted to see it come alive again. He was doing it in memory of his father. He wanted to come and play eighteen holes and think of him. Giving up at this point would be admitting to failure. He'd rather go bankrupt. If he was going to fail, then why not fail hugely?

He had convinced himself that Bridget should be off limits. Her appeal should be resisted. But watching her, he was reconsidering his declaration to himself. Why not pursue a satisfying physical relationship with her? It would take the edge off their business differences. Would she be a willing participant, or would she insist on maintaining a respectful professional distance?

"Come. The team is meeting in the club house."

She followed him and he held the door to the new space. It was the only building onsite that he had been able to design from scratch. They had demolished the old clubhouse and sited this one in a better location to take in the grandness of the course.

"This building is new. We needed a clubhouse that could host large press gatherings and an influx of fans for important tournaments."

She stopped in the center of the space and glanced around.

"It's an architectural feat," Will said. "Its design showcases the course, but the expansive space is inviting."

He couldn't tell what she was thinking, but he needed to take it slow with her. His general manager had warned him that the North family had taken losing this place to heart and shortly thereafter, her mother had died. It was complicated involving her. Maybe he was asking too much.

"This building houses a conference center for meetings or training." He led her away from the main open area and to a secluded private section that housed the meeting rooms.

Walking into the conference room, he heard his four-person executive group, which had already begun a heated debate about the renovation of the hotel. The conversation stopped when everyone noticed he had brought a guest.

"This is Bridget North. She is a marketing executive that I was bringing in for Breen, but I thought she may be able to help us with The Donne."

Alex was the first to stand and hold out his hand to her. They sat at the conference table and each member introduced himself.

"One odd coincidence that I'd like to mention is that my father, Thomas North, was a previous owner of this resort years ago. I had a front-row view of some of the challenges of trying to bring back an old but loved relic."

There was no sentiment in her tone. It was professional and honest. It was the combination of her beauty and professionalism that had softened them.

Alex said, "William mentioned scheduling a meeting with your father for later today."

"Yes. My father loves this place, but that feeling couldn't be translated to a sound business plan. I'd imagine that it will take a logical approach and not intuition."

Merle said, "It's important to understand the

history of this place, so we don't fall victim to some of the same mistakes."

William directed the accountant, Jeremy Spire, to give a review of recent expenditures. The rest of the project meeting was fast-paced and he made sure to keep everyone on task. Bridget was given a list of objectives, and their Communications Director promised to set up email and passwords for her to their company site.

As they were walking out, Will asked her, "Did you bring different shoes?"

Glancing at her, he remembered their walk through the park at night. She was impossibly sexy with her long legs and four-inch heels. Why did she wear such impractical shoes? There was no way he could walk the course with her.

"I didn't know I needed flats."

"We're at a golf course." He wanted to get outside and show her the course.

Alex chimed in. "Upstairs the supply room has begun taking in stock. Maybe you can find her a pair of women's golf shoes?"

William said, "It's worth a shot."

Bridget said goodbye to everyone and they went up the stairs to the professional shop.

"Do you know your size?"

"I've never worn golf shoes, but I'm a thirty-seven typically."

Pulling out a box of shoes, he handed them to her. "A gift."

She sat on a bench and reached down to remove her shoes. His blood pressure skyrocketed. He had seen her sexy stockings and knew what was underneath her skirt.

Turning away from her, he made a point of checking out some of the other items that had come in. They would be able to open nine of the holes for golf within a few weeks.

"I'm ready." She looked just as sexy in golf shoes.

He accompanied her outside without saying anything.

***

William turned towards her and his muscular chest and then his piercing gaze caught her attention. Bridget pushed away thoughts of kissing him. The erotic encounter at the park intrigued her, but she would be smart to think about her professional life. No good would come of letting down her guard and throwing herself into his arms. She had been given an opportunity to build her career, and she couldn't allow an affair with William to drag her down.

"You're lost in thought." His voice drew her back. He was impossibly sexy and was standing much too close.

She stepped away and took in a deep breath. "The changes here are incredible. It doesn't look like the same course."

He moved toward a cart.

She pulled her hair back into a ponytail. "Could we walk instead of using the cart?"

"Absolutely."

She didn't want to sit next to him in the golf cart. She needed distance and a physical distraction.

They started towards the ocean. "Are you an avid golfer?" He was athletic and seemed drawn to sports.

He was wearing reflective sunglasses, so it was impossible to get a read on him. "I don't play at a competitive level, but I'm considered adequate."

She silenced her instinct not to ask personal questions. "What drew you to this place?"

They kept walking. "I was having a pint in Dublin and overheard a few men say this place was cursed. I had remembered coming here with my dad and playing the course several times. It was where I learned to play."

She stopped and turned to him. "So you knew this place was a challenge before deciding to invest? Or did that drive you to take the risk?"

"I'm not interested in methodical or easy. I want to succeed at things that are difficult."

They continued walking and she thought about his answer. Why did he seek out risks? Was it to prove his worth? Or did he enjoy the adrenaline rush? Olivia had told her that he was into extreme sports. The more difficult, the better.

"Nothing is certain, but the sheer size and scope of this project is daunting. I intend to breathe new life into it. I'd like to play this course occasionally and think of my father."

His admission surprised her. It must have been tough to lose his father at such a young age. He had been seventeen years old and the media had discovered Olivia as the forgotten daughter. She'd read about his family after their brief encounter at the gala. She had been unfair to him, but the grief surrounding her own mother's death had been on her mind and she had blamed Oliver Bolles in some tangential way. He had been the one to make a comment to her father about purchasing the old relic. Her father had insisted that the great Oliver Bolles must have some inside knowledge. The comment had led to years of struggle and disappointment for her family. The stress had been too much for her mother's fragile health.

He was several steps ahead of her. "Do you play golf?"

She needed to hold on to some happy memories and not be sucked into a discussion about the struggle of this place. "No. As a small child, my grandparents would take me to miniature golf, but that never translated to an actual love of the game."

He laughed. "I don't think mini putt-putt courses qualify as golf."

"Did you play miniature golf as a child?" She should probably stay away from questions about his childhood.

She waited for his answer, but her eyes were drawn to the ocean in the distance.

"No. My father started taking me to actual golf courses at five years old. It didn't matter that the age limit was seven or eight. No one told him no, and I learned to play."

The sun was warm, but the wind coming through the course cooled everything. The course had changed tremendously and walking it with William gave her the chance to enjoy the slow pace of the day and collect her thoughts. This place didn't hold the same power over her anymore. She no longer felt it had defeated her family. Somehow, the changes and the intervening time had washed away the feelings of loss and defeat.

She could see that huge machines had changed the terrain. "That is an extreme sand pit."

William looked over the landscape and ran a hand through his hair. "It needs to be challenging. For The Donne to survive, it has to become relevant again."

She turned towards him. "So you're hoping to appeal to both the professionals and the tourists?"

He had a way of looking at her that made her thoughts about the business hard to access. "Hopefully the committed amateurs, as well." Everything about him was so intense and made her think of his qualities as a man and not the marketing campaign.

The sound of the machinery caught her attention. It had hit a solid surface and the engine sounded labored.

"There are gigantic rock formations just below the surface. We should head back, or we'll be late for lunch with your father."

They walked back over the sweeping lawns, being careful not to disrupt the work that was happening.

"I'm not sure you need any advice. You made it sound as if this project wouldn't finish, but it looks to be well underway. And your management team seemed ready for any obstacle or challenge."

"The budget is the issue. We'll complete it, but the costs are out of control. We need to lessen the labor and the machine costs."

He opened the door to the Land Rover.

She said, "I don't know if my father can offer any advice. That was his issue as well. But he didn't think about the money, only the goal."

William placed his hand on her arm. "I've found

that it is worth having conversations with the previous owners. It's impossible to predict what advice or comment might be helpful." He stepped back and said, "Don't worry. I won't push him. I know it must be hard."

He closed the door and walked around the vehicle. Bridget mused over the new sides of William she saw today. He was an interesting mix of absolute force and empathy and understanding.

***

After a short drive, William pulled up near a stone pub that was within walking distance of her father's new cottage. Tom must already be inside. He was probably already on first-name basis with the owner.

They walked into the pub and she scanned the bar for her father. He was sitting at a table speaking with a waitress but stood and walked over when he saw her.

He wrapped her in a tight hug. "Bridget, sweetheart."

She hugged him and then stepped back. "Tom, I'd like you to meet William Bolles. William, this is my father, Thomas North."

William reached out and shook his hand, saying, "It's a pleasure, Mr. North."

"Tom. No one calls me Mr. North."

They followed her father back to his table and the waitress came over.

"I'd like the house stout."

"A water, please," Bridget said.

They glanced at the specials board. William asked, "Do you have any recommendations?"

Tom said, "You can't go wrong with bangers and

mash. But they offer plenty of options."

Bridget looked at the menu and decided on a salad, but when the waitress came over; she ordered a chickpea stew. Both her father and William ordered the bangers and mash, and she handed the menus back to the server.

Her father wore a striped polo shirt with baggy shorts. "I couldn't believe it when Bridget told me that her new boss owned The Donne."

William smiled and nodded. "The connections between our families are interesting."

Tom said, "It's odd the way things turn out. Your father once told me in passing that he thought the locals should take over The Donne and bring it back to life. I get lots of advice, but in this case I took it. It's strange now that his son owns the place."

William's head jerked back. "Did you know my father well?"

Tom lifted his glass mug and took a sip. "No." She shook his head. "Everyone in this part knew who he was, but he didn't often speak with the riffraff. It was a comment over a pint."

Bridget stayed quiet and thought about the chance meeting years ago.

Tom continued, "I was at a wedding in a fancy hotel and escaped to the bar area for brief time. A conversation came about and he turned to me and said something should be done about the old course. He had remembered going there, but it had fallen into disrepair."

"My father enjoyed coming to Ireland."

Tom nodded. "The Bolles family owned an old manor house here and he would come often."

William shifted in his chair. "Tom, getting back to The Donne. Have you been by recently?"

Her father shook his head and took a sip of his lager.

"I'd like to give you a tour. We hired a firm a year ago to redesign the course and increase the difficulty level while keeping some of the key elements. I'm trying to get one of the major events to use the course."

Tom sat up straighter. "It was plenty difficult."

William smiled at her. "The idea is, to attract outsiders, it needs to host a major tournament. If this is achieved, then professionals will come. This area is stunning and increased tourism would help the local community."

Her father leaned forward. "I wish you luck. My partners and I tried for years to salvage the place. I'd spend time there and feel a connection to the history, but in the end it only brought misery."

"Why misery?"

Bridget intervened. "I don't think we need to bring all of this up."

"It's fine," Tom said. "I was convinced the harder I worked, it'd eventually pay off. If I gave up I'd be throwing away everything I had worked for. I should have seen that I didn't have the resources to make a go of it."

The waitress brought their food and asked if they would like another drink. Her father declined and William asked for salt.

"All businessmen fail at some point," William said. "It's the lessons learned from the failure that move you forward."

Tom shook his head. "I gave it five years of my time and energy. My wife died shortly after the bankruptcy, and I realized that I had neglected my family."

William lowered his voice. "I'm sorry about your wife. You must miss her greatly."

"She was my one great love and always believed in me. That was why it was so hard."

"If you're willing to come to The Donne," William said, "I'd like to get your opinion on a few of the problems we're having."

"You don't need my advice. I didn't know what I was doing." His admission surprised her. Usually he insisted on explaining how he could have done things differently. Maybe he'd finally moved on and didn't want to go back?

"My guess is that you learned a tremendous amount about the place. One of the issues is that the local laborers don't want to work on the course and we have to bring machinery in from far away. The cost is much higher."

Her father looked down at the floor. "I can't help you with that."

William met her glance and then looked at Tom. "Why are the locals so reluctant to work at The Donne?"

She had never heard him speak about a resentment of the locals. For years, it had been where weddings would take place and important events would be celebrated.

Bridget asked, "Tom, I've never heard you say that the locals refused to work there. Why would they?"

Her father touched her hand. "Bridget, it's not for me to say. The past should be left alone."

"I have a thick skin," William said. "Don't worry about insulting me."

Tom studied him a moment, then said, "There was a scandal involving your father. It's the Bolles name. I don't know that people trust it."

"What type of scandal?"

"Your father seduced a local widow and left her pregnant. It was about the time that he gave me the advice to purchase The Donne, but at the time I didn't know about the scandal."

"Why would people care all of these years later? Relationships fall apart for many reasons."

"The area surrounding The Donne is a small community. The widow, Meredith Blair, was a schoolteacher and her husband had died the year before. She had fallen in love with your father and then found out he had a family. He had lied to her. She had her child and had to live with the shame of it."

***

William sat back. He couldn't believe that Tom North was telling him about another infidelity. Meredith Blair had never approached the family or the media. Maybe the story wasn't accurate? "I'm not sure what to tell you. I've never heard of this."

"She and her son moved away years ago. But it tarnished the Bolles name. The family closed up the manor house and as far as I know, they haven't been back."

Why hadn't any of his business executives heard of this? The food he had eaten was beginning to churn uncomfortably in his stomach. His father had betrayed the family another time. It would cause a renewed interest in the scandals surrounding the family.

"How many years ago did this happen?"

Tom North was trying to come up with a date. William made himself relax his tight fists. It happened a long time ago.

"Less than twenty years ago but not by much. Bridget would have been eight or nine years old."

Did Bridget know about this? He glanced at her and she touched his forearm.

"It doesn't make sense that this type of gossip would continue unabated."

Tom let out a long sigh. "It's the name. Bolles. In this area, scandal is not forgotten and the family is judged."

He stood and motioned for the check. "We should go. Thank you for sharing this information."

Tom stood. "I'm sorry for your troubles."

William handed the server a few bills without looking at the bill. "I'll be touch. You should come and take a look at the course."

He shook Tom's hand and walked out of the pub. Was this why most locals had refused to work with his firm? Why only a few would and then overcharged for their services?

Bridget joined him on the sidewalk. He needed to be alone, but would take her home. He headed to his vehicle and she followed him.

Tom North was a nice guy, but he had no idea of the bombshell he dropped. The pieces were beginning to fall into place. He hadn't known his father spent so much time here. He thought it had only been an occasional holiday.

Parking near Bridget's flat, he hoped she would get out without a word.

"You should come in for tea. You're in shock, William."

He ran a hand through his hair. "I'm not. Believe it or not, this is not that unusual."

"That's not true. Finding out you have another sibling, a further connection to your father, is life-changing."

"It hasn't been proven true." Meredith Blair had never approached his family. If it were true, why hadn't she reached out for help?

She touched his shoulder. "Come inside. Please."
***

Bridget watched as he shut the engine off and undid his seatbelt. What could she possibly say to him that would help? It was a terrible way to learn that he had a sibling. Was there a decent way? Being an only child, she had no experience with siblings, but she had felt a longing for someone to share a family history with. Maybe this young man would bring William joy, or maybe he was rotten and would be a disgrace.

Her stomach tightened and she climbed out of the vehicle. He was in shock and needed her help. She couldn't send him home to Mrs. Blake yet.

Walking with him up to her flat, she motioned to the small sitting area and went to put the kettle on. Why did tea help when someone was in shock? Maybe it was the ritual. Something to do with your hands.

She brought him a mug and placed it in his hands. He sat on the edge of the rose-patterned sofa. William looked out of place in this outdated flat.

"Are you angry?" He looked as handsome as

ever. She had seen photographs of Oliver, and William looked like his father. His straight nose and blue eyes were the same, but William had a stronger jawline and darker hair.

He met her gaze. "I've experienced a range of emotions in the last hour, and yes, anger is among them."

Bridget bit her lip. "I'm sorry this is happening."

He held her gaze. "Did you know?"

She shook her head. "No. I asked my father while you were leaving the pub why he hadn't mentioned it to me. He didn't think it was important. It wasn't until you were asking why the locals would be reluctant to work at The Donne that it occurred to him that you didn't know."

William placed the cup on the table. "I had no idea that my father had another relationship, nor did I know that his family owned a manor house here. I'll have to ask my aunt and uncle."

"The child couldn't have been more than a year or two old when your father died. Maybe Meredith Blair thought it was best to leave the situation alone."

He threw up his hands. "And then not say something for all of these years? I've been living in Ireland for five years. I bought The Donne two years ago. My family couldn't tell me the truth?"

Bridget tucked a piece of hair behind her ear. "Maybe they didn't know. You father must have been good at keeping secrets."

He stood up and turned away from her. "If they owned a house here, then a servant or someone would have mentioned it to them."

She glanced at his striking profile. "You may find

that you like Meredith and her child."

William turned back and shrugged. "She may have remarried and wants nothing to do with the Bolles name, and will want to shield her child."

Nodding, she said, "The boy must be eighteen or nineteen."

He looked at her. "Your father said it was a boy?"

She nodded again. "Nothing needs to happen today. Take some time and think about how to approach them. You don't owe anyone an explanation. In the end, this is a reflection on your father, not on you."

"I should go."

Bridget stood up and gently touched his arms.

He reached forward and pressed his lips to hers in a fleeting kiss. "I appreciate your kindness around this. I'll talk with you tomorrow."

He was unguarded and vulnerable. Tomorrow he would regret that she saw him like this. It had to be painful. It reminded her of how horrible she had been to him when they had first met. Why did she expect so much from him? He was a Bolles, but had been just a child when his father had caused so much heartache.

Chapter 8

A few days later, Bridget got an early morning text from William that he'd meet her at The Breen Hat Company.

Walking the few blocks over to Breen, she thought about the issues facing the hat company. The Operations Manager had quit the previous day and the place was in turmoil. Her days had been spent checking in with Patrick Breen in the morning and then working on the marketing plan for the golf resort with William's executive team.

William had even extended an offer of employment to her father, and Tom was busy organizing the pro shop. But Breen couldn't exist on an influx of capital without a plan to move forward. The employees were on edge, having become fearful of the anticipated changes.

Passing through the gate by the side entrance, she saw William waiting for her. He was dressed in a cycling shirt and jeans that showcased his athletic form.

When she got close to him, he said, "We have to make a few decisions today. Apparently, Breen is unable to function without input from us."

She remained calm. "It does seem a little unfair to

purchase the company and then not give them any indication of future changes."

He ran a hand through his hair. "They're not even on my radar. I have no plans. Hopefully, you do."

She assumed he would micro-manage every decision, not take a step back. "I haven't immersed myself in this company, as The Donne has taken all of my attention. But with the marketing elements coming together over there, I can focus on Breen."

"They need your calming presence."

Bridget repositioned her handbag on her shoulder. "I need some direction from you."

She met his gaze and awareness swept over her. She had been trying so hard to block out her attraction to him, but the merest glance and she nearly melted.

He relaxed his posture. "You understand the overall investment and goals. They need to reorganize the main business functions so they're breaking even within the year. And you'll need to hire an operations manager."

"Are you coming inside?" She stood waiting for his response.

"No. I expect you to manage the crisis and have a working plan. Call on the members of the executive team if you need help. We can talk about the specifics tonight."

She wanted to argue with him and insist he take more of a role, but she remained silent.

"Good luck. You definitely will be able to manage this on your own. I'd just get in your way."

She smiled. "Good luck with your day."

Turning away from him, she walked into the factory. William was giving her a ton of freedom. She had attended the dinner in London and had met the couples that had placed their money with him. She helped him convince them that it was a good investment, revamping The Breen Hat Company. If the business didn't turn around, they would lose their investment and the employees would lose their jobs.

The receptionist greeted her politely and, after calling upstairs, sent her up to the executive offices. The shop floor was oddly quiet, and she felt her stomach tighten. Had others left as well?

Climbing the steel staircase, Bridget was careful not to catch her heels. She opened the fireproof steel door and walked into the office space.

Patrick Breen greeted her. He led her into his office and closed the door.

"Thank you for coming, Ms. North. We've been waiting for someone to come and tell us what the plans are."

She took a seat by his desk and waited for him to sit. There was an overflowing stack of papers and other items covering the entire desk. "We have to develop a plan together. I've been caught up with setting the marketing plan for another business, but now I'll be transitioning to Breen."

Patrick Breen shrank behind his desk. "I've been trying to rescue the company for a few years. I don't know how to proceed. And I didn't know how he wanted the money to be spent."

Did they not handle their accounts or pay payroll? "What do you mean?"

Patrick fidgeted with a pencil. "I couldn't use the funds to pay payroll. What will happen when it runs out?"

She pulled a file out of her bag. It held the legal documents and she remembered seeing a schedule of disbursements. "The purpose of the money is to keep Breen afloat and only ten percent was disbursed. You should pay your workers."

He wrung his hands. "The money is in the account. But without permission, we didn't know to proceed. Should we cut salaries? What type of budget will be implemented?"

She stood up. They were a disaster. "You should instruct payroll to disburse any owed monies today according to the established pay rates and salaries. I'll start working on a budget with your operations manager."

Patrick Breen shook his head. "As I told you on the phone, he left yesterday. He couldn't take the stress."

Bridget looked at him. "Should I call him or would you rather hire someone else?"

"That is up to you, Ms. North."

She shook her head. "No. I don't know him. William Bolles purchased Breen because it is a good, solid company that makes a quality product. He understands it will take time to resurrect the business, but you need to take a role in helping that happen."

He threw his hands up. "I don't know what to do, or I would have done it."

She kept her voice neutral. "Let's get your operations manager back. Let him know payroll is guaranteed for the foreseeable future. I'll assemble an executive management team meeting for Monday so decisions can be made. In the meantime, I'll begin looking at the budget."

Patrick stood up and shook her hand. "Thank you, Ms. North."

Breen needed new management. Patrick was not a leader and he was too worn out to have a vision. "I'm going to spend the day here and interview different employees. Let me know what your operations manager decides. I'll use the conference room?"

William had her working nonstop on the marketing plan for The Donne and now he expected her to swoop in and solve the problems here. The issues were complicated by global economic pressures, and not related to small adjustments in product or inventory. It was beyond her expertise, but somehow she would find a path forward.

She met with the accounting clerk and went over the vendor invoices that needed to be dealt with, and then asked for a report of what Breen was owed by couture houses and boutiques. When she asked about marketing, she realized that they relied on word of mouth and reputation. Maybe she could make a difference in helping them promote themselves.

The overall attitude was somber, and she was exhausted after being an optimistic cheerleader all day. William arrived at four thirty in the afternoon and the shop floor was desolate. Bridget was doing a walk-through with the Patrick and the operations manager, Brian Feeney, and watched William walk onto the shop floor.

He wore an exquisite suit and her heart gave a jolt when he smiled at her.

***

Breen reminded him of the old world. The older generations would make things by hand, and the shop hadn't updated with new processes or technology-driven machinery. It needed to be revamped or the work shifted overseas, but neither Olivia nor Bridget would agree. He had called Olivia a few hours ago and she had given him her rationalization for keeping this place in Dublin again. It made sense. The skill and expertise was here, but it would require an enormous undertaking to bring them current.

Walking over to join Bridget, along with Patrick and another manager, he acknowledged to himself that he had missed her today. He was getting used to her rapid-fire questions and her continual pitching of new concepts and ideas. He looked forward to interacting with her throughout the day and watching her solve issues or negotiate tough decisions.

The greatest challenge had been not showing any reaction to her physically. He enjoyed watching her fashionable parade of skirts and dresses. He had never taken an interest in women's clothing, but she was different. She was feminine and captivating with her curious looks and generous smile.

She had earned the respect of his management team with her well-presented ideas. But if he acted on his desire, it could create an awkward dynamic for everyone.

"William, this is Brian Feeney, the operations manager, and you already know Patrick Breen."

"Gentleman." He shook their hands and glanced at Bridget.

"Why don't we head to the conference room? I'd like to discuss a few ideas." He placed a hand on her lower back and waited for the owner and manager to head upstairs.

He leaned towards her. "I would imagine you have a few ideas of your own."

"I do, actually." She held his gaze and he wanted to push her up against a nearby steel column and capture her mouth. But instead he moved away from her. He needed to refocus his mind or he would get upstairs and not have a coherent thought.

He decided not to sit down in the conference room. "Breen is a viable company. You have a sought-after, high- quality product in a niche market. However, your social media and marketing presence is nonexistent. You also need to update your shop floor. Ms. North will help you find the right consultant to drag Breen into this century and she will oversee the revamping of your marketing presence."

His lecture was met with silence. He didn't look at Bridget. She would soften his words and slowly bring them along.

Patrick Breen began to explain why change was not a good idea and William silenced him with a movement of his hand. "This is not up for negotiation. If you want Breen to survive, then you need to reinvent yourselves and the company. If it's something that you don't support, then resign."

Bridget stood up. "William, everyone supports the overall goal of modernizing and increasing brand awareness. But the individual steps of how we will get there need to be figured out. Over the next few months, we intend to take each small challenge and make progress towards the overall objective."

He glanced at her. "As long as the change is met with enthusiasm and positive support."

His words were met with silence. "We have

another engagement tonight, gentleman."

He shook both men's hands and waited for her to gather her belongings.

Walking out, she said, "That was harsh."

He held the door for her. "I saved both of us hours of tedious conversation. Either they show a willingness to change or they should be encouraged to retire."

Her voice was matter of fact. "It needed to be approached in a gentler way. I know they need to change, but they have fifty or sixty years of combined experience. You can't throw that away."

Meeting her gaze, he said, "You can spend time speaking with them and slowly bringing them along. But I wanted them to realize that they needed to support your ideas and embrace change."

He walked with her to his Porsche. She was too much of a distraction to take her back to his place; instead he would take her out to dinner.

Bridget had slipped behind his defenses, but he would resist her charm. Life was to be lived, and he had no interest in settling down. He had every intention of continuing to seek out adventures and push himself to new levels. He was not about to invite someone into his life that would want to rein him in.

***

Bridget was wrung out emotionally and wanted to retreat to her flat. The Breen employees held so much worry and anxiety about the future of the company that the weight of it sat heavily on her shoulders.

"Let's go to Temple Bar tonight."

"Without reservations, I doubt we would get in."

William pressed a button and with a voice

command, dialed the restaurant. Within moments, it was arranged and he navigated heavy traffic through the city.

Temple Bar drew tourists and those with deep pockets. The neighborhood was charming with cobblestone streets, art galleries, and architectural splendor.

He shifted gears. "Did you want to stop by your flat to change?"

She glanced at him. "Do you mind waiting?" Most men didn't have the patience to wait.

"No. I have a few calls to make, and I can catch up on emails."

Bridget nodded. "It was a stressful day. It'll be good to change. The fear and worry is palpable throughout Breen."

He double-parked so she could get out. "If that doesn't shift, then I doubt Breen will survive the year."

"Twenty minutes?" She was pushing her luck, but she wanted to shower and dress in something less work-related.

"I'll wait." He was getting Alex on the phone when she closed the door.

Running up the flight of stairs to her flat, she tried to let go of the worry. She had the entire evening to ask him about his plans for Breen and to try and get information out of him. She wanted to help resurrect the company. More than fifty employees were depending on the outcome. Some had been with Breen for years and years and knew little else.

Bridget stepped into a hot shower and lathered with lavender soap. She could already see a path forward for Breen. With a reimagining of their marketing materials and presence, she should be able to help them gain market share. They were a known quantity with a superior product. The issue was the cost. It was a reality of doing business that most products could be made cheaper in faraway places.

Drying off, she brushed out her hair and only lightly blow-dried it. William was waiting. She found a short black couture dress that she had picked up at a sample sale a year ago, but had only worn once or twice. Finding patterned silk stockings, she quickly dressed and then put on four-inch heels. She hoped that she didn't look too stylish for a business discussion, but dressing up was a welcome distraction.

She picked up her clutch, added her keys, and then touched up her makeup before heading downstairs. It had been just over twenty minutes, and she saw his metallic gray car across the street.

Waiting a moment for the traffic to stop, Bridget ignored two university-age men that called out to her. They were obviously harmless and on their way to a pub, but she didn't want to offer any encouragement.

Climbing into the car a moment later, she had the impression that William was withdrawn. Was it the waiting or his phone conversation?

He gripped the steering wheel tightly and jammed the gear lever accidently.

She smiled at him. "Did I take too long?"

He focused on the street. "No. I spoke with Alex and Merle."

"You seem distracted."

He met her gaze. "It's the dress."

"I don't understand."

Why would her dress bother him? It was

appropriate for going out. It was fitted and had a satin band at the waist and a deep-V illusion neckline with a lace bodice and tulle inset.

"You wore it the night we met."

She thought back to the gala and tried to visualize what she wore. It had been this dress. She had been exhausted when she arrived home, but the practical part of her hung up the dress and climbed into bed wearing an old shirt.

"Does it bother you?"

He started the powerful car and pulled out into traffic. "I can remember the first moment I saw you."

It was odd that he remembered what she wore. Men didn't, usually. Her father never had a clue about her wardrobe or the importance of a particular dress. She remembered coming downstairs for breakfast in a nightgown and her father saying she looked nice.

"Have you forgiven me for being rude that night?"

"There is nothing to forgive. You were merely expressing your opinion."

"I'm protective of Tom, and for some reason put tons of meaning into a throwaway comment. In the end, my father was responsible for his decisions, not yours."

Bridget smoothed down her dress. She should have worn something else.

"Why do you call him Tom and not papa or dad?"

She held onto her pendant necklace. "It started when I was a teenager. My mother worked all the time and I looked after him. Sometimes I would have to fetch him from the pub and I hated the way bystanders would look at me when they realized he was my father. I started calling him Tom and he didn't object."

***

Bridget surprised him at each turn. When they first met, he had assumed she was a beautiful party girl without any real responsibilities. She had seemed confident and unreachable. He was beginning to figure out that it was a façade she cultivated to keep others out.

"That must have been hard for you." He reminded himself that he needed her involvement in the business and not to make the mistake of getting involved with her personally. Unfortunately, she had a way of getting under his skin. He was fascinated by her. The way she walked into a room, or the things she decided to question or even the empathy she showed to others. But he needed to block out her beautiful body, her kind nature, and her inquisitiveness.

"It wasn't perfect, but I had parents who loved me. I'm grateful for that."

He turned onto a side street. "My parents split up often and the ups and downs were tough to manage."

She gave him a heartfelt look. "Have you been able to connect with your brother?"

"I have a private investigator working on it, and so far it seems to be a truthful account. I've seen a picture of the teenager and he's the spitting image of my father and Olivia."

"What's his name?"

He resisted telling her, then realized everyone would soon know. "Oliver William Mancini."

"His mother called him Oliver? I don't know that I would have done that."

"It's loaded, but she must have thought he was going to acknowledge his son, but within months he died in a motorcycle accident." He slowed the car and looked for parking on the street.

"Have you met his mother?"

He nodded. "I met her briefly. She works as a librarian about four hours from here." The press coverage around it would need to be carefully managed. It'd bring up old scandals and gossip.

"Will she allow you to see Oliver?"

He stopped near a parking spot and looked over his shoulder. "She had a paternity test conducted when Oliver was born and my father was refusing to acknowledge him. I'm trying to determine the authenticity of the testing. Apparently, she decided not to pursue legal action against the estate."

She lowered her voice. "But you and your sisters have missed out on getting to know him."

He maneuvered the car into the parking spot. "When my father died tragically, she decided to raise the child on her own. But it's had a downside. He isn't keen on meeting me or my sisters."

He shouldn't be telling her all of this. He doubted that she would disclose the information, but it was muddying the waters. He was allowing the relationship to veer into a more personal connection.

He turned the engine off. "Can you walk a few blocks?"

Bridget laughed. "On pavement or cement."

She met his gaze and he remembered walking with her through the park. He had never been drawn to high fashion, but she was slowly changing his mind. The exquisiteness of her sexy stockings and dress heated his blood and made him want to explore her body.

He leapt out of the car and walked around to help her onto the sidewalk. In her heels, she reached his jawline. It would be so easy to pull her into his arms and lose himself in her embrace. Did she want the same, or did she want to keep their relationship on a professional level?

Placing his hand on her lower back, he drew her slightly closer as they passed a group of people.

He opened the door to the restaurant. "Have you been to Temple Bar before?"

"No. I'm excited to visit such an iconic place."

They were shown to a secluded table and several patrons watched her every move. She looked happy and ready to enjoy the evening. The problems at Breen today were pushed to the background. He should resist bringing up the failing company.

***

Bridget opened the elaborate menu the waiter handed to her. She tried to distance herself from the desire she was feeling. Nothing good would come from giving in to the attraction building between them. She had blocked out her first meeting with him. It had been so embarrassing, she wanted to crawl under the table thinking about it. He had brought out the worst in her. It had been the milestone of her mother's death that had triggered the response, but she found it difficult to forgive her emotional outburst.

William put aside the menu. "Are you thinking about a strategy for Breen?"

She looked up at him. "Not exactly. But I should be. It will take some new thinking, but it can be turned around."

"Do you think Patrick Breen is too set in his ways to change?"

She contemplated her response. She didn't want to rush to take action without fully understanding all of the elements. "We may need to take a longer-term view and see how he responds to requests for change. He's been in survival mode for a number of years, trying to hold on until the economy improves."

He took a sip of water. "As the leader, he needs to be able to predict the future."

She smiled at him. "That's a little unrealistic." His standards were too high.

His eyes narrowed on her and her body began to heat. "Running a company and keeping it profitable takes many strengths. Strengths he may not have."

It was nearly impossible to concentrate with his gaze piercing into her soul. "Don't expect too much at the start. Removing him would only worry the clients and employees further. If he can become part of the solution, then the company will be better off."

Their waiter appeared with the bottle of wine and went through the ritual of offering William a taste. The young man poured them each a glass of the expensive vintage and retreated quietly from the table.

William raised his glass to her. "To success, Bridget. May this project provide enough challenge to keep you interested, but not so much that you give up."

She took a sip of the delicious wine and thought about his words. She wouldn't give up, even if it was tough. "What happens if Breen can't be turned around?"

William glanced at the specials board. "I'll sell the rights to manufacture the product to an overseas venture and recoup as much of my investment as I can."

"How could you start this process with a plan for giving up? Don't you care what happens to the employees?"

He met her gaze. "I absolutely care. But the world is constantly changing, and they need to be ready for that and not insulated from the risk. If Breen can't turn a profit within the year, then it should be closed."

She tried to keep her voice even and controlled. "So, you're saying that you might fail?"

"I don't see selling or reorganizing a business unit as a failure. Failure would be doing what Patrick Breen has been doing. Continuing on the same path, yet expecting different results."

She thought about the families that relied on the company. "I want to see Breen succeed and keep manufacturing in Ireland."

He took a sip of wine. "I'm not surprised. You're Irish and knowledgeable about the industry. It's why you were chosen for the role."

What if she did fail? What if no matter what she tried, the economic realities were against her? A shocking realization struck her——she was getting into a similar situation to the one her father had embarked on all those years ago. She would need to be less sentimental and more practical if she hoped to make the right decisions. She didn't want to let employees go, but she also wouldn't try to save a sinking ship. She had to be smarter than that.

"I'm starting to think that I'm in an impossible

situation."

"You'll have the full cooperation and expertise of myself and the management group. These odds are the reason that there's a huge profit to be made."

"What if we don't agree on an important element?"

"I'll give you a ton of freedom, but ultimately I'm responsible for making the tough decisions."

She would not just follow along blindly. "What if you're wrong?"

Her question was met with a brief silence. Then he leaned forward and said, "You'll be tasked with carrying out an order that is incorrect or flawed."

He might be charming, but he was also confident and overbearing at times.

Her toughest work might be with him, and not Patrick Breen. "How collaborative are you?"

He met her gaze. "Collaboration has a place in leadership, but at some point decisions have to be made. I'm open to ideas and willing to give my team the freedom to make mistakes, but ultimately I'm going to weigh in on crucial decisions."

She could also be collaborative, but wanted to be in charge of the vision for Breen. She had no desire to carry out dictates from someone offsite who thought they knew best. She wanted his help; she wanted him to be part of the process.

"Do you want to order?"

She nodded. Glancing over the menu, she selected trout with a dill sauce.

The waiter appeared and took her order, then William's order for filet mignon and Brussels sprouts.

He refilled their wineglasses and disappeared.

She took a sip of wine. "How do you see this unfolding with Breen?"

William sat back. "We need to give a briefing to the management team and decide on a path forward. The brainstorming stage is unscripted, but once a plan is put in place, then you will be expected to make that happen and report back frequently."

Bridget smoothed a stray piece of hair behind her ear. "What if the team takes the wrong approach? How much collective experience in the fashion world do your executives have?"

"You may not like a decision, but only if there is a compelling reason to reconsider will that happen."

***

He watched her process his comments. Bridget had the intelligence and depth to run a successful company, but she was also headstrong and would need to learn to take direction. Unfortunately for him, he didn't care about Breen; he was far more interested in her.

"Your father seems to be settling in at the golf course. According to the manager, he spends the better part of each day in the Pro Shop."

She nodded. "He's happier than I've seen him in a long while."

They chatted more easily until the food was served; his filet mignon was cooked to perfection, but he barely tasted it.

A memory surfaced of the first time he set eyes on her. He had felt something catch deep in his chest. He didn't believe in love at first sight. He had learned early on that women could be vindictive and self-centered. His own mother was famous for presenting a certain image to the world, yet making their home life a living hell. He had missed his father terribly during those periods, but somehow Oliver would always return.

"I don't think you've ever mentioned your mother." He watched a veil come down over her emotions.

Bridget held onto her pendant necklace. "It's been nearly a dozen years since her death, but I still miss her."

"Tell me about her."

She glanced away. "I'd rather not talk about her."

"Why? I've found that speaking about my father now is helpful. It allows me to put some of the memories in context." It allowed him to honor his father's legacy. He was able to discuss the good things that Oliver had done and not just the troubling behaviors. His father had been an immensely good guy; he'd been concerned about those less fortunate and often did charitable acts in secret.

She neatly cut a small piece of trout and placed it in her mouth. "I don't need to justify my memories."

He reached across the table and placed his hand over hers. "You were young when she died. Certainly an adult lens would help you put things in perspective."

Bridget placed her fork down. "What are you referring to? What do I need to put in perspective?"

"The night we met, you accused my father of wreaking havoc on your family. You said that a comment he made to your father carried so much weight that your father acted on it without regard to anyone else. Were you speaking about your mother?"

Why did he need to push her on this issue?

"My mother loved my father and would have supported anything he wanted to do, even if it was the wrong thing." Why was it so hard for her to see her mother as a living, breathing person who may have made flawed decisions?

William waved the waiter away. "Did she think that he shouldn't invest in The Donne?"

Bridget shook her head. "I don't know. She didn't share her thoughts on the subject. Instead she kept working harder at menial jobs to compensate for his dreams."

"Maybe she shared those dreams?"

"I doubt it. She was the practical one. The one who always picked up the pieces when everything fell apart."

"Maybe she chose that role for herself?"

***

"Did your mother play a part in your father's deceptions?" She was being unkind and unfair, but couldn't stop herself.

William held his hands up. "Yes, she did. By being emotionally unavailable to him. So he sought connections elsewhere. He was responsible for his actions ultimately, but she had a part to play."

His openness surprised her. Why would he choose to admit his parents' shortcomings to her? Maybe by admitting the issues, he could distance himself?

"What type of relationship do you have with your mother?"

William ran a hand through his hair. "It's at times difficult and at times fine. She expects too much from me, and so I distance myself. There are other times that I enjoy her company."

He was lucky to have a mother in this world. "I've seen pictures of her in the media. She's a very beautiful woman."

The restaurant was bustling. Bridget glanced around and realized she had enjoyed herself and had even let her guard down a slight bit.

William signaled for the check and the server cleared the table before bringing the bill.

Stepping onto the cobblestone, William pulled her closer and said, "I'd like you to come back home with me this evening."

She could see desire building in his gaze. He was giving her a choice. Did she want to act on their growing attraction, or keep herself in a firmly established professional role?

"I don't know if that's a good idea."

He pulled her away from the crowded sidewalk and into an alley near the restaurant. Reaching forward, he lightly touched her face before capturing her mouth in a demanding kiss. His body shielded her from the street, and the only thing she could see was him. Her eyes closed and she enjoyed the feel of his tongue exploring her mouth.

Reaching out, she grasped the lapels of his suit jacket and pulled him closer. His warmth enveloped her and she was lost. William placed a hand on the stone building behind her and used his other hand to hold her head steady and he explored her mouth fully.

Breathless, she pulled back slightly before seeking his mouth again. Her growing desire caused warmth to spread throughout her body. She wanted to go home with him, but her rational mind kept throwing up obstacles.

"Come home with me, love."

"It would complicate things."

He placed both hands on either side of her head and looked into her eyes. "Complications can be good."

She didn't want to turn him down. What if she stepped out of the impossible standards she set for herself and just gave in to desire this once? Would it be such a bad thing? Could they maintain a professional distance?

"I'd want you to keep it a secret."

He physically retreated from her. "If we embark on an affair, then it has to be out in the open."

She touched his arm. "I don't want others to know that we're crossing business and personal boundaries."

He faced her fully. "You're overthinking this. It's not anyone else's place to have an opinion."

She wanted him to take her in his arms again, but was it worth the risk? Would others judge her?

"I can't, William. I'm sorry."

He walked with her back to the Porsche without saying anything. She couldn't risk her professional life. She needed the respect of others if she was going to make a difference at Breen. So why did she feel lost?

She wanted a physical relationship with William. It had been almost two years since her last relationship ended badly. Her boyfriend at the time accused her of being married to her career. But she needed the security of knowing that she could provide for herself and help her father. She couldn't go back to the feeling of powerlessness that poverty had instilled in her. If it hadn't been for her mother's sister, she would have never had a chance in the fashion industry.

He drove through the city streets without saying a word until he pulled off onto a dark side street adjacent to a park.

"Why are we here?"

William turned off the engine and opened the first few buttons on his shirt. "A compromise, of sorts. A few stolen kisses can remain our secret."

Her blood heated watching him. He removed his suit jacket and tossed it in the back seat. Excitement skittered over her skin. What did he intend to do?

William turned and ran a hand up her leg until he stopped at her dress. "I've spent the entire dinner thinking about your stockings."

"Why?" Women wore stockings. Why was he so intrigued?

"You're incredibly sexy and I wanted to see what you have on under your dress."

She wanted him to continue his exploration, but he was waiting for her. What did he want from her?

The small enclosed space and leather seats wouldn't allow her to move closer to him. She wanted more from him. A heightened awareness settled over her.

He lightly touched the edge of her dress and her senses went haywire. She wanted him to explore her body fully.

"I want you to touch me." His low voice encouraged her.

She reached forward and touched his rigid length.

She squeezed lightly and heard his indrawn breath.

He moved his hand from her dress and held her chin as he kissed her properly. She moved closer to him, but the gearshift prevented her from fully climbing into his arms. She should have gone home with him. They would be in a proper bed and not trading kisses in a confined space.

William moved his hand and caressed her breasts through her sheer dress, finding her erect nipple and applying just the right amount of pressure. Shifting in her seat, she undid his belt clasp before finding the zipper. He moved and undid the button for her before capturing her mouth again.

Pulling back, he said, "I want things from you that are not possible in this space."

She explored his length more fully and released his zipper so she could enjoy the feel of his smooth skin.

He moved his hand back to her silk-covered legs and pushed aside her dress as his mouth sought her neck. She could barely hold still as his hand pushed past the silk of her stockings and caressed the bare skin at the top of her thighs. He pushed aside the scrap of lace covering her and she could feel moisture pooling inside of her.

He lightly stroked her feminine core and she shifted her legs to give him more access. He groaned into her neck and she began to rhythmically stroke his length as desire built inside of her. She was beyond caring that they were in a car parked beside a park. Somehow the darkness gave her courage.

He pushed a finger inside of her and she nearly leapt off the seat. "Focus, love."

She couldn't focus, and her body was hot and reactive. She tightened her hold on him and was rewarded with a surge of desire spiraling inside of her. He kept stroking her, winding her tighter and tighter until he traced her lips with his tongue and then simultaneously plunged his fingers inside of her while he explored her mouth. She felt a hot liquid explode over her hand as she shattered into a cascade of pleasure.

William kissed her neck. "I can't get enough of you." He retreated from her and straightened his clothing.

She adjusted her dress, but her body was sensitive and pleasure-soaked. She'd remember this erotic encounter forever.

He started the car and she reached for her seatbelt. "I can see why you prefer stockings to pantyhose."

She had never considered the easy access that stockings would allow. For her, it was about comfort and a heightened fashion sense. But she wouldn't put them on again without thinking about this encounter.

They were at her building within a few minutes, and she said goodnight and climbed out of the car. It was odd: she could barely look at him, but moments ago they had been intimate. Would she regret acting so out of control tonight?

He murmured, "Sleep well."

"Cheers, William." She closed the heavy door and turned away.

Bridget bit her lower lip and walked into her building. She would need to face him tomorrow over a conference room table with his entire executive team looking on. She should have been so much more reserved with him. She wasn't the type of person that took unreasonable chances.

Chapter 9

Bridget slipped a stack of files into her work bag along with her laptop. Stepping out of her flat, she pulled the door closed and locked it with her key.

She lingered at the top of the stairs for a moment. Her building housed mainly working professionals, and she rarely encountered anyone.

Walking down the flight of stairs from her flat to the street, she thought about the challenges facing Breen. It wasn't yet seven o'clock in the morning, so she would arrive as the doors were unlocked.

An understanding of the overall business was emerging, but she had questions about the financial management of the company. Their budget included only minimal marketing efforts; instead they relied on word of mouth. They were shipping a decent amount of product, but the company accounts continued to show a loss each week.

Bridget greeted the security guard that opened the factory and he held the door for her. She walked through the shop floor and up to the executive offices.

She nodded to Patrick Breen, who was already in his office. The remaining offices were still dark.

Leaving her laptop and handbag in the conference room, she went to speak with Patrick.

He stood up. "Good morning, Bridget. I'm surprised to see you so early. We've been putting in long days."

She sat down in the wooden chair facing his desk. "Yes, and there is more to do."

Patrick rubbed the back of his neck. "I'm nervous about all the change."

Bridget crossed her legs and leaned back. "The world has changed and Breen needs to adjust some of the long-standing business practices."

Patrick meticulously rolled up the sleeves of his blue pressed shirt. "But in some ways, nothing has changed. We make high quality, hand-stitched hats."

She took a deep, calming breath. They had had the same conversation many times. He believed that it all came down to producing a quality product. "Yes, Breen makes beautiful hats. And you're concerned that the changes won't improve sales or the bottom line."

Patrick turned in his chair to look out the window. "I know that resisting change is not the right thing. But if I agree to the changes, I could be wrong about everything."

Bridget allowed his words to be met with silence. It was true, they could be making the wrong changes.

Patrick held his hands over his heart. "This company is my life."

She needed to show deference, but at the same time encourage change. "You must be willing to bend or grow. It's not about the quality of your products. That's the only reason Breen is still around. It's about reaching new markets, reducing costs, and stimulating demand."

Patrick turned to face her. "I can't control those

things, but I can control the product."

She nodded. "Change can be done in small, incremental ways. And the quality of your products will not be comprised."

He picked up his pen. "This process is harder than I imagined it would be."

Bridget stood up and said, "Change is hard, but the alternative is even harder."

Patrick reluctantly smiled. "You're right about that."

Walking out of his office, Bridget greeted three of the employees who worked in purchasing and sales. After helping herself to coffee in the small break room, she went into the conference room and pulled out the marketing documents. She had received proposals from three marketing firms and needed to present her vision to William and the other members of the Maglia Rosa team.

***

The next day, William disconnected the call from his mother and climbed out of his Land Rover. The golf course was close to being completed, and looking out over the rolling hills to the sea brought him pleasure. Not as much pleasure as a few nights ago, possibly.

His thought about Bridget. She was captivating and sexy. He wanted her in his bed, instead of settling for mindless stolen kisses in a car or elsewhere. She clearly intended to keep her professional life separate from her personal relationships. And he had no interest in a secretive affair. He was not his father. He hadn't been able to come up with a reasonable solution yet.

William walked into the conference center and

began to organize his thoughts. He had maybe an hour before his team arrived. Checking his schedule, he decided to go to New York the next week for a gala his mother was organizing. It was better if he didn't let too much time elapse between visits. He had learned years ago that it was better to face an issue head-on than allow it to fester.

He wanted Bridget to come with him. Maybe spending time away from Dublin would allow them to figure out a compromise.

William called his assistant and confirmed his schedule. He requested that a private jet be booked for the trip to New York. Bridget could be counted on to stand up to the bitter woman. She was the perfect date to bring to the gala. She adored the fashion world and was confident enough to walk into any room.

Pulling up the recent projections on The Donne, he went through all of the financials, and the small amount of improvements on spending gave him some hope that the project wouldn't be a complete loss. Somehow, having Thomas North involved had softened the local community.

William had mentioned to different locals that he was aware of the scandal from years ago and was seeking out the woman who had reportedly had his father's child. He would need to tell his sisters, but first he wanted to meet with the boy.

The management team began to arrive, and he asked Bridget, "Can we have a private chat?"

He led her into another meeting room and closed the door. "Do you want to talk about what happened the other night?"

She shook her head. "No. Not particularly."

Dressed in a slim-fitting grey dress with a narrow belt, she looked every bit a fashion executive.

He sought out her gaze, but she looked down at her hands. He said, "I'd like a repeat."

She drew in a breath and a fleeting smile tugged at her lips. "It wouldn't be smart."

He crossed his arms. "Maybe. But I'd like to strip off your dress and take you against the wall right now."

She met his gaze. "It was a mistake."

He kept his tone neutral. "How so?"

She gestured towards him with her hands. "I work for you. I can't let myself become the woman who sleeps with her boss."

He stepped forward and lightly touched her shoulders. "So, if I fire you, then you'd feel free to indulge me?"

She shook her head. "I don't want the shame of being fired, William."

He pulled her closer. "There has to be a way to work this out. Breen needs your expertise, but there's this tension between us that we can't ignore."

She moistened her lips. "You could compromise and be willing to keep any connection between us private."

He had no desire to repeat his father's mistakes. "You're ashamed of being in a relationship with me?"

Her voice didn't falter. "Not if I weren't employed by you. But it looks odd, and then when it's over, it'll be even more awkward."

He'd rather have her in his personal life if he had to choose. But would she be satisfied? "We can keep it private from our business associates for now, but I insist we not hide it from our families."

She looked away. "That sounds impossible. The members of your executive team are like family to you."

He kissed her neck. "I'm traveling to New York next week and I'd like you to come. There's a high-profile gala that will attract much of the fashion world that I'd like you to attend as my guest. Olivia and Fionn will be there. You can work on Breen marketing, and I'll take care of a few loose ends."

He pulled her closer. He could feel a pulse beating erratically in her neck. "Also, I'd like you to play nine holes of golf with me after this meeting."

She pushed away from him. "Fine. But I'd like you to keep the professional and private interactions separate for now."

He opened the door to the corridor and watched Bridget walk to the conference room. She was getting to him. Her demand was actually what he would normally practice——keeping his business and personal life separate. But he didn't believe in indulging in an affair with a business associate. Bridget was different. He craved her in a way that he refused to dwell on. They would get to know each other better and somehow a solution would present itself.

Alex pulled out a chair for Bridget. "We should start with the golf course and other company matters, and do Breen last so we can spend most of the meeting on it. Does that work?"

***

Bridget reviewed her notes and attempted to push away thoughts of William. She wanted her presentation to come off without a hitch. She had spent three weeks at Breen and, with Jeremy, created a set of financials and narratives to explain what was happening and where the company needed to go.

Throughout the meeting, William challenged his managers to come up with solutions and not just issues. They seemed more positive on the golf course, and when the discussion turned to marketing, Alex invited her thoughts.

A lively debate took place, with William deciding to call for a vote. They agreed five to one on a direction for the marketing campaign for The Donne and moved on.

William said, "Bridget, can you give us a briefing on The Breen Hat Company?"

Bridget stood and handed out copies of the financial and strategic plans. "I'm trying to figure out how they react to changes in the marketplace. They have a highly regarded product, but the pricing has remained stagnant for five years. It has to do with pressure from overseas pricing. The work is going to be around marketing initiatives and getting them to produce some of the components elsewhere. There's a fear of failure that's pervasive, and it's taken a toll on employee morale."

Alex asked, "Is there a change of leadership needed?"

"I don't think so. Patrick Breen is nervous about too much change, but he's willing to take some risks. I'm hoping that we are able to translate the risks into measureable results."

Merle said, "It's better to figure out the issues before jumping in and making massive changes."

"Bridget, thank you for putting all of this together. Jeremy, you as well. There is a sufficient amount of orders coming in, but they are losing money. The employees are paid an average wage. I'd like to know why there is a gap."

She said, "The owner is a perfectionist, and if something isn't to his standards, then it's scrapped."

William twisted a pen in his hand. "Do they keep track of those costs?"

Bridget shook her head. "Their system was ancient and everything was kept in hand-written journals. We've hired a cost accountant and slowly the accounts are being computerized."

Straightening in his chair, William said, "I'd like you to find out how much material they are writing off."

"We have begun keeping track of scrapped material and much discussion has come up around why things are scrapped. There's a huge potential to shift the practice."

Her business insights impressed him. She understood how to see through problems and look for solutions. But how could they possible work together if he pursued a relationship with her?

***

William stood and said, "I'm traveling next week. Shoot me an email if something comes up."

The men around the table stood up and gathered their materials.

William traded a few remarks with Alex and Merle.

Arlo said to her, "Well done, Bridget. It's difficult to step into a company and figure out how to help them move forward."

She smiled. It had been an interesting few weeks. She was finding her place at Breen. Going to work each day no longer felt odd or uncomfortable.

"Bridget, let's head to the pro shop and see if Tom can locate a set of clubs for you."

Alex said, "Ah, you've found new blood. Bridget, be careful. He's known for asking for allowances."

She laughed. Placing her laptop in her bag, she walked with everyone up the modern staircase to the open foyer.

Going into the Pro Shop, she saw that the space was filled with open boxes. The inventory was in the process of being unpacked, and displays were partially assembled.

Walking over to a box of golf shirts, she pulled out a lime-green shirt and inspected the quality. She ran her hands over the seam and was impressed with it.

Coming back into the room, Tom said, "I was hoping to catch sight of you. The hat place is doing without you today?" Her father looked happier than she had seen him in a long time.

She gave him a brief hug. "William has asked me to play nine holes of golf. Does the shop have a set of clubs I could use?"

Her father smiled. "I'll get a set for you."

"If I'm to help with the marketing at all, I need to at least have a glimpse of why golfers would want to come."

"The course is challenging. You may discover a new passion." Tom disappeared into the back room.

She had discovered a new passion, but it was better if she didn't say anything to her father. He was overjoyed when William asked him to help out in the pro shop, and she didn't want him to worry about any awkwardness in the future if she and William had a falling out.

William changed into dark blue shorts and a white golf shirt. He looked confident, and she wondered how the afternoon would play out.

Glancing over her shoulder, she said, "I should check in at Breen today."

He gave her a wide grin. "After we play, I'll drop you off. But you have spent long days there the last few weeks; maybe an afternoon off isn't a bad idea."

Tom walked back in with a set of clubs.

William asked, "She'll need shoes—and do we have any women's apparel set up yet?"

Tom said, "Yes. I have to look through a few boxes."

She took out her phone and called Patrick Breen to let him know that she was going to take the afternoon off. She needed to let her mind process all of the feedback she received today before she introduced the ideas to the Breen management.

Her father came back with a feminine-looking orange golf shirt and a white skirt, along with shoes.

She took the new items of clothing and went into the women's locker room. The space was on the main level and reminded her of a well-appointed spa. Glancing around, she took in the soft muted tones and high-end finishes that created a sense of luxury. She opened the door to a steam room and smiled. The design team had created a space that was inviting.

Hanging her clothes in a locker, she changed into the golf clothing. Her father hadn't given her socks, so she left her stockings on. She had not the slightest idea of how to play the game, and didn't welcome the idea of being at a disadvantage.

Walking back into the pro shop, she found William going over the clubs with her father and tried to appear relaxed and ready for the challenge.

William smiled at her. "You look the part, love."

She smiled at her father and he gave her a quizzical look. William acted much more interested than a mere boss would be and she hoped her father wouldn't pick up on the subtle hints.

"Wish me luck." She leaned forward and kissed Tom on the cheek.

"You won't need luck. You have a master player to show you the ropes."

Stepping outside, an excitement washed over her. It was interesting to try something new. She hoped that she had some of her dad's natural talent with golf. The sun was bright overhead, but a wind was coming off the ocean, keeping everything cool.

William had a cart waiting outside and they placed their clubs in the back. "I'm going to take you over to the driving range before we start. It'll give you a chance to try out your swing."

Riding to the other side of the hotel gave her a view of the construction underway. There weren't many people on the course this afternoon, and they were the only ones at the driving range.

He went over some of the basics, and she watched him take a few swings. Stepping into the platform, she placed the ball on the center of the mat and thought about her stance. After a few practice movements, she swung and hit the ball.

"You clearly have hidden talents, Ms. North." She smiled at him and lined up another shot.

William took shots as well, giving her the chance to try different clubs and get a feel for hitting the ball. Several times, she caught him watching her, and she could feel a fluttering in her chest. Attempting to break the spell, each time she focused on hitting the ball.

He placed his clubs back in the cart, and after taking a last swing, she did the same.

Driving back over to the course, William said, "The first hole was designed to be challenging on this course. It requires an iron. I'll go first and then show you how to set up for the shot."

Parking the cart, they climbed out and brought their clubs over to the tee-off area. His swing was practiced and powerful. The ball landed far enough away that it was barely visible as it bounced onto the green.

Looking around the sloping hills, she could see they were alone except for golfers far down range.

He handed her an iron from her bag and said, "Place your feet here, shoulder-distance apart."

Looking down the hill and out to the sea, she hoped that she would replicate the swings she had on the driving range. William stood behind her and placed his hands over hers on the club, showing her how to gradually swing. She could feel him touching her from her legs up to her shoulders. It was impossible to concentrate. She was hypersensitive to his touch.

"Focus, love." He was messing with her. She pushed back against him and could hear his indrawn breath.

He stepped back and she took the swing,

narrowly missing the ball. She lined up her shot again and attempted a second swing. The ball moved half the distance of his shot.

The afternoon continued with him showing her how to swing and her hitting the ball with inconsistent shots. It was so frustrating.

Looking at him, she said, "Are you tired of playing with me?"

He leaned forward towards her and her breath caught. "I'm finding your approach fascinating."

She needed to distance herself from him or she would become a quivering mess. "We are not well-suited. You must have been playing since you were ten years old."

He lowered his voice. "Four. It was one thing that my father and I could do together."

Bridget concentrated on her body and followed all of the corrections he had made to her form. Instead of touching her, he stood back watching. She blocked him out and took a swing. The ball made it halfway to the green.

He gave her a wide grin. "Excellent shot."

Climbing back into the golf cart, she asked, "Why did you ask me to play?"

He drove the cart closer to the green. "I thought we could talk about Breen, but I hadn't realized you had never played."

He must have assumed with her father's involvement at the golf course that she played often. "I was in school when he tried to make a go of this place and it put a terrible strain on my mother. So, I wasn't keen on hanging out here."

Their interactions took on a predictable pattern.

He was intent on teaching her the game and his patience didn't falter. But with each swing she became more aware of him. He was no longer a sexy entrepreneur that she could hold at a distance; she was getting to know everything about him. His thoughts, approach to life, and his charm were breaking down the barriers she had steadfastly erected around her emotions.

They approached the ninth hole and she began to show a tiny amount of improvement. Relief flooded over her. The wind had kicked up, and she found that she had to tie her hair back.

***

William watched as the wind blew her skirt and he could see the top of her stockings. Didn't she believe in socks? What was it about her that he found so fascinating? He understood the tension between them, but he was equally fascinated by how her mind worked and how she challenged him intellectually. They were going to disagree about Breen, and she wasn't going to back down, but instead of feeling bored or irritated, it intrigued him. She cared deeply about others and it allowed her to reach something inside of him that he kept hidden.

She took a shot and he watched the movement of her body. "You're a fast study. But putting is a different skill."

When her ball made it to the green after several attempts, he walked up behind her and touched her shoulders. "Relax your body. This part of the game is not about power, but control. Letting the tension leave your body will help you place the ball in the hole."

He steadied her hips and could hear her indrawn

breath. "I can't putt with you standing so close to me."

He wanted to bury his mouth in the curve of her neck. "You need to be able to block out all distraction."

She turned and pushed him away. "I'll get it in with one putt." It took four and she was frustrated enough that she wanted to walk away. She didn't like to lose, but he found that quality rather endearing. He wanted to distract her by pulling her into a tight embrace, but he needed to give her time.

He enjoyed her company and adored watching her learn the game. "Let's make this a weekly outing."

She met his gaze. "I can't take an afternoon off each week."

"Long work hours are necessary, but you should be able to find time to play nine holes."

Patrick Breen needed to be let go for the company to move forward. He was giving Bridget time to come to that conclusion by herself, instead of insisting on immediate changes. She had an idealistic sense of what was possible. But maybe she would coax Patrick into the current century.

"I'll drive you back to your flat. Come over for dinner and we can discuss your plans for Breen at length."

She shook her head. "I don't think that is a good idea. The other night got out of control."

He moved closer to her. "Our work week is intertwined. You'll have to get over the awkwardness."

A look of stubbornness settled over her. "We're playing with trouble. It'd be far better if we decided not to indulge our fantasies."

Why did she resist the attraction between them? "I don't agree. Life is about fantasy." He pulled her close and she resisted briefly.

She whispered, "Not here. Anyone could see us."

He kissed her neck. "You're too prim. Life is to be lived, not hidden away."

She pushed him away. "What if my father were to see us?"

He couldn't worry about other people's reactions. "Neither of us is in a relationship. We have the freedom to explore a romantic involvement."

***

Stepping away from him, she said, "It's fine for you. You're not from here and you don't care what others think. But I do."

She placed her golf clubs back in the cart and waited for him to join her. He was looking out towards the ocean and seemed not to be in a hurry to leave. It was an enjoyable afternoon, but their disagreement weighed on her. She wanted to explore the desire between them, but nothing good would come of it. She would be left with a tarnished reputation and he would move on.

***

By the end of the week, Bridget was on edge. She had spent long days at Breen trying to unwind the reasons the company was failing. Part of it was the international pressure on prices, but some of it had to do with the fear the employees had around change. They thought that the business was about to go under and couldn't be drawn into any type of enthusiastic approach to trying something new.

She had been avoiding William, but had agreed to

meet him for dinner that evening. She didn't want to go to his house, but he had insisted and it would have become a point of contention if she didn't agree.

She needed to maintain a distant demeanor and insist that their relationship stay on a professional footing. But unfortunately, images of their recent sexual encounter kept surfacing in her mind. They were focused on their careers, but allowed their desire to surpass everything.

Looking through her wardrobe, she decided to avoid stockings and instead put on slim-fitting jeans and a pressed white dress shirt. She dabbed on a touch of makeup and added a few bracelets and a necklace. William had offered to pick her up, but she insisted on taking public transportation.

Arriving at close to seven o'clock, she walked up the path and twisted the antique door chime.

Mary opened the door. "It's lovely to see you, dear. William is on the terrace."

Crossing through the great room, she relaxed her rigid shoulders. She hadn't seen him in a few days and worried that their attraction would block everything else out.

Stepping through the double doors out onto the stone terrace, she stopped. He was on the phone and in a heated debate about foreign markets. He motioned for her to come out. He ended his call and a silence hung between them.

He looked sexy in a light blue, short-sleeved dress shirt tucked into worn jeans with bare feet. He seemed relaxed and, after meeting his gaze for a moment, she looked away. She had missed him over the last few days, which was crazy. Her job took every ounce of her energy, and yet she found time to fantasize about him.

Stepping forward, he captured her in a fleeting embrace and kissed her cheek. "I wondered how long you would avoid me." Her heartbeat accelerated.

Moving away from him, she leaned on the low stone wall. "It was a hectic week at Breen."

He smiled at her. "What would you like to drink?"

"Red wine, please."

He went into the house and she forced a breath into her lungs. When he had ended his call and met her gaze, all thoughts evaporated from her mind. She wanted things from him that were impossible.

***

Returning with two glasses and a bottle of Cabernet Sauvignon, William reminded himself to take it slow. She worked for him, and his fascination with the beautiful brunette wouldn't help move his companies forward. The markets over the last few weeks were volatile, and the grip he had on his investment portfolio was beginning to slip. He needed a win.

He opened the bottle of wine and poured two glasses. He watched her take a small sip of the full-bodied wine and tasted it himself.

"How did you make out this week?"

She turned away from him and looked out at the back garden. "It's been difficult. The employees are fearful of change, and they are, as a group, exhausted by all of the financial issues facing the company. Most of the long-time employees have stayed, but the younger ones have jumped ship. They took any energy and momentum out of the place."

He took a swallow of the boldly flavored wine. "Your new hires will be critical."

She met his gaze. "I'm worried the doom and gloom atmosphere will infect the new employees."

She had the ability to be a great manager. "I've faced similar dynamics. You may need to ask a few people to leave if they are unwilling to help turn things around or unable to accept the changes coming."

She nodded. "There are some positive aspects. The quality of the hats is remarkable. With a shift in marketing, increased sales won't be a huge obstacle. Also, raising the prices slightly will help the bottom line."

He sat down in a teak chair. "What's going on with the owner?"

She met his gaze. "Patrick. I've been able to figure out that he's the inspiration behind the product line and overall quality, but he is pessimistic and seems defeated."

William took another swallow of wine. "I'd offer him an early retirement."

Bridget touched the stem of her wine glass. "He isn't ready to leave."

Working with his team, the hardest issue that they faced was deciding when to let someone go. "He may never be ready. Some owners need to be forced out."

She took a sip of wine. "The employees hold him in high regard and genuinely care about him. Removing him would have a negative effect on operations."

He had missed talking with her. "Letting him stay beyond his usefulness will only hurt the company."

"I don't agree. Patrick Breen does have something to offer."

"You're responsible for implementing the strategy we agreed upon and helping to insure Breen becomes profitable. If Patrick Breen is hindering that process, then you don't have a choice."

She met his gaze. "We owe it to the longtime employees to help them make the transition."

William ran a hand through his hair. He didn't want to spend the evening debating the best approach to saving the garment company. "No. Actually we don't. We owe it to our investors to turn the company around and begin making a profit."

Bridget placed her wineglass down on the table. "I'm not sure the two are mutually exclusive. Re-energizing and supporting the team already in place may produce better results."

He agreed with her approach and thinking. "Just be careful that you're not coming from an emotional place, wanting to save the employees from the natural consequences of their actions."

Mary interrupted. "Dinner is ready," the older woman said, and then without waiting for an answer, returned to the house.

Bridget inhaled deeply. "I'm not coming from an emotional place, but it is worth thinking about the social fabric of the company. It ties into loyalty and commitment. Both factors will help the company re-emerge as a successful business."

He stood up. "Let's have dinner."

Opening the door for her, the soft musky scent of her perfume enveloped him as she walked past. He had had a difficult time all week pushing thoughts about her aside. He had thought about their golf game, and how much he enjoyed watching her learn the game. She could barely play, but he found that endearing instead of frustrating. He had evaluated the way she approached learning a new skill and had been impressed. Instead of becoming self-conscious or irritated, she threw herself into the game, and at times laughed at her inability; at other times she concentrated hard to gain the needed skillset.

Pulling out a chair for her, he asked, "Have you spoken with Olivia this week?"

"No. I know Olivia would give me advice if needed, but we have more of a working relationship then a friendship."

He sat opposite her. "Do you need more of a sounding board for this project?"

She shook her head. "Not while I'm trying to get my bearings. Possibly when I need to make decisions on key elements of the marketing or promotion."

Mary served her special meal, rack of lamb with potatoes and roasted vegetables. He could tell what his housekeeper thought of his dinner companion based on the effort she put into the meal. She adored Bridget.

He said, "Thank you, Mary. This looks delicious."

Bridget thinly sliced a carrot and took a bite. "How was your week?"

He met her gaze. He was close to bankruptcy and needed to borrow heavily to survive. "Complex. Several of the companies I have under management need additional investment to get to the next level. I spent most of the week dealing with the financing issues."

As he took a bite of the well-prepared lamb, she asked him, "Are you overextended?"

He stopped himself from choking. He was careful to keep everything afloat. "Somewhat. Owning various struggling businesses is challenging, and much of it comes down to forecasts and luck."

She placed her fork down. "Some of the elements must be out of your control?"

He hid the reality of his situation from many onlookers, but not his executive management team or investors. His father had dismantled any real wealth the family had, and he had been clawing his way out of a deep, deep hole. "I come from a family that had vast resources but my father had squandered most of it on bad investments and responding to scandals. I took a modest portfolio when I left University and increased it tenfold in the last seven years. But the challenges right now are significant." In fact, if something didn't shift soon, he would need to contact his brother-in-law before his reputation began to take a hit.

Bridget pushed her long hair behind her shoulder. "When you took on investors to purchase Breen and didn't allocate the funds yourself, it made me realize that you were probably overextended, but didn't want to tell Olivia no."

He nodded. "It can be smart to share the risks. But with the golf course bleeding money, I have to be careful of tying up other assets."

She took a sip of wine. "I know that you're successful, but there must be limits to your resources. The golf course itself is a money pit."

"I knew that going in. It was more of a

157

sentimental investment. I love to play the course, and have many happy memories of spending time with my father there."

She softly said, "It's surprising that you don't have more resentment towards your father."

What good would resentment do? "Maybe if he lived I would have, but I lost him when I was only seventeen. I'd have done anything at the time to bring him back."

She nodded. "Children love their parents, even if they're imperfect. But you should be careful of taking on the world in defense of him. He was larger than life and an easy target."

His body tensed and he attempted to relax his rigid muscles. "He did make himself a target."

Her gaze seared into him. "Do you feel the need to defend his reputation?"

He shifted in his chair. "Yes. There are countless naysayers who think they know something about my father, but they don't."

She said in a soothing tone, "You were a child, William. They may know more than you do about his life."

He placed his napkin on the table. "No. I knew my father and he was a good man."

***

Her heart went out to him. "He must have loved you very much. But don't feel that you have to defend his every action."

His held his hands up. "He's not here to defend himself and I don't think anyone should speak ill of the dead."

Bridget placed her napkin on the table, leaving

her dinner half-eaten. "I believe that one should speak ill of the dead, if it's the truth. It doesn't negate how much they were loved, but by acknowledging the truth, it short-circuits the need to defend something that can't be defended."

His nostrils flared and his eyes narrowed. "So you would have me admit publically that my father was a disgrace?"

She sighed deeply. "Yes. His enemies will keep pushing for the truth until it's given. By acknowledging that he made mistakes, you take the power away from those who would like to see you fail."

He shook his head. "By acknowledging his failures, I'll be giving them ammunition."

"It doesn't work that way. It takes a considerable amount of effort to defend a lie. Let go of trying to defend his reputation. He was human. You'll always have your memories of him and those don't need to be shared. Acknowledging the truth will put you in a much stronger position."

Bridget thought about The Donne. Playing the course with William and seeing her father happy there had shifted her dislike of the place. But there were memories to contend with. The place had fallen into bankruptcy the year her mother died.

William stood up. "Your father wasn't a businessman and got in over his head. It wasn't his fault the place fell into bankruptcy. But my father caused an unbelievable amount of heartache."

She pushed her chair back and stood. "My father dragged the family through years of struggle and loss trying to make a go of that place. It led to his drinking issues."

William crossed his arms. "Plenty of people have financial issues and don't take up alcohol to compensate. My guess is that your father would have had an issue with drinking whether he was successful or not."

The loss and failure was painful. But William was right. Tom also drank when he was happy. Her father was in a good place and she hoped it would continue.

He ran a hand through his hair. "Maybe we should take a walk."

"How about a bike ride? Mary told me that you keep a spare bike for guests."

He smiled at her. "Typically for male guests, but I have one Olivia has used. Are you an experienced cyclist?"

She crossed her arms. "I've ridden quite a bit, but these days do more cycling classes than actual riding on the road."

"I'll organize the equipment. If you go and find Mary, she can find you suitable clothing."

In one of the spare bedrooms, Bridget changed into black biking shorts and a lime green reflective shirt. The clothing fit her perfectly, and she wondered if a previous girlfriend had used the outfit.

She met him in the driveway, and he asked her, "Do you want to ride around the city or head out to a rural area?"

"Maybe a city route?" It had been years since she had ridden in Dublin.

He had changed into grey biking shorts and jersey, revealing a toned and muscular body. Even though he worked insane hours, he obviously kept himself in top physical condition. She found an adrenaline rush as he guided a bike toward her. It was a high-end frame and he had adjusted it for her.

He handed her a helmet. "Good?"

She nodded and watched him climb on his bicycle. He adjusted his helmet and balanced for a moment before heading out. She followed him through the old streets and began to relax. She enjoyed the views of Dublin at night. He took her through Dubh Linn Gardens, and she pushed herself to keep up with him. After thirty minutes or so, he increased the intensity and she had to concentrate to keep the bike moving at a decent clip. Her tired muscles began to revolt as she caught sight of his house.

Following him into his uncluttered garage, she climbed off the bicycle and waited for him to place his bicycle onto hangers so it was suspended from the ceiling.

He ran his eyes over her. "You did well."

She gave him her bicycle. "You make it sound like a test."

He laughed. "Some people are serious about cycling and some are more tourists wanting to meander around. You were a pleasure to ride with."

He stepped towards her and she considered his words. He was clearly interested in a physical relationship, but had no interest in protecting her privacy. It would not serve either of them.

"Don't overthink this, love." He lifted the hair off of her shoulder and kissed her neck.

She pushed against him and enjoyed the feel of tight muscles. "I need a shower."

"You taste amazing." He drew her into his arms

and captured her mouth, deepening the kiss, and she could feel her body flood with desire. This was not a smart move.

He traced her lips with his tongue before plunging back into her mouth, demanding a response. She clung to him and returned each kiss. After several minutes, they were both breathing hard, and he said, "Come upstairs with me."

She stepped back. "It would complicate everything. It's not a good idea." Moving away from him, her limbs were uncoordinated and she had to resist the temptation to throw herself into his embrace. She would tarnish her reputation and it would be hard to recover from that. The world hadn't changed much. She would be judged and he would walk away without censure.

He brushed a stray hair from her face. "Do you ever throw caution away and enjoy the moment?" His low voice drew her in.

Taking a breath in, she said, "No. I learned a long time ago that it's not the way to a safe, productive life."

He was standing so close she could see deeply into his eyes. "That's what motivates you? A productive life?"

She wanted to lose herself in his embrace. "If you want something to happen between us, then you need to promise me that it will stay our secret."

He became still. Would he choose to indulge in a secret fling or demand that they tell the world?

He lightly touched her cheek. "I don't like secrets. They're poison."

She ran her hands over his chest and enjoyed the

feel of his masculine body. "Neither one of us is in a relationship. I'm not suggesting that we lie to anyone." She waited for him to decide.

William touched her neck and drew her into a slow, sensual kiss. Her body heated and she clutched at his shirt.

"Come."

He led her through the back part of the house. Opening a wooden door, he guided her into a dark room and said, "I'll handle Mary Blake. You can turn the shower on, if you like."

He disappeared, and she clicked the door shut and turned on a lamp. The room had a masculine feel. It was William's bedroom, and not a guest suite. There was an artistic rendering of a bicycle on the far wall and an elaborate walk–in closet that held suits and cycling apparel.

The bathroom was through another door, and she turned the shower on. She was making a mistake. What if others found out that she had an affair with her boss? They were both single and unattached, but it didn't change the fact that she worked for him. She could quit and beg Olivia to take her back.

She heard him come in. "I said goodnight to Mary and she's going to bed. I'll be able to sneak you out later."

Why did she have such an issue with the concept of sneaking around? She was the one who wanted to keep their fling a secret. But if she was proud of her choice, then she wouldn't want to hide it.

"Why haven't you gotten in the shower?" William took off his shirt and she stared at him. He began to remove his biking shorts and she turned away.

"Why don't you go first?"

He laughed. "Spoilsport."

Leaving the bathroom, she went in search of a bathrobe. She located a terrycloth robe in his closet and stripped down, putting her borrowed clothes in the hamper. William would need to find her clothing later.

He emerged from the shower, drying off and then securing the towel around his hips.

She walked by him and he reached out and tugged her close. "I was hoping that you would join me."

"It felt too intimate to take my clothes off in front of you and get in the shower."

He touched her chin and tilted her head up. "Are you having second thoughts? I can take you home if you're not sure about this."

She looked into his eyes and her heart accelerated. "I'm sure. I just need a moment to shower."

Pulling out of his embrace, she walked into the marble bathroom and closed the door. He had left the shower running for her. Hanging the robe on the back of the door, she climbed into the warm spray and soaped her entire body. Rinsing the lather off, she turned off the shower and stepped out. She took a white towel from a bench near the shower and dried off.

It wasn't smart to leap into an affair with him, yet she wanted to lose herself in his embrace. He was compelling and maddening in equal measure. Her body was drawn to him and her instincts told her that he would be hot and intoxicating. Her limited experience hadn't been earth- shattering, but after their encounter in the car, it was obvious they had incredible chemistry. She had fantasized about him each waking moment.

She ventured out of the bathroom and discovered that he was gone. Standing in the middle of the room in a towel, she wondered if he had second thoughts. The door opened, and he came in wearing jeans and carried her clothing, folded in a neat pile.

Why was this so awkward? "Have you changed your mind?"

"I thought you might have, so I fetched your clothing."

"I haven't."

He placed her clothing on a nearby chair.

"I know you have concerns about getting involved with me because of our professional relationship."

Bridget held her arms tightly against her body. "I want to pretend that doesn't exist tonight."

He stepped closer to her. "If you want to take our relationship beyond a night of passionate sex, then you need to acknowledge the truth."

Her head jerked back. Was he throwing her earlier words back at her?

"I'm not trying to score points. I want you to be sure about this and not just allow yourself to get lost in the moment."

He was right. If she was going to do this, she had to be honest about it.

She moistened her lips. "I want you. It doesn't matter to me that we work together or even that it might be discovered. I'm willing to acknowledge it."

He opened his arms and she threw herself into his embrace. He captured her mouth in a slow, sensual kiss. Her heart accelerated and she held onto his shoulders to steady herself.

William moved a hand down and tugged her towel off. She gasped at the sudden exposure to the air.

"You're beautiful, love." He glided his hands down her back and pulled her bottom closer to him. She could feel his hardness through his jeans and her insides melted.

He left her mouth and placed delicate kisses along her jaw and then her neck. She unbuttoned his jeans and he drew in a deep breath.

"I'm losing my mind." He picked her up and placed her on the bed before disappearing for a moment into the bathroom. He came back with a few foil packets.

"You remind me of a warrior. Your muscles are sleek and defined."

He laughed and removed his jeans, leaving them on the floor and putting the protection on the bed. His body was masculine and hard-edged, with no excess weight.

"Slow can be good in this case." He captured her restless hands and pinned them above her head. He took his time tasting each of her breasts and coaxing each nipple into unbearable tightness. She moved her body and he released her hands and held her hips in place as he slowly kissed each inch of skin between her breasts and feminine core.

She ran her hands through his hair and tried to distract him from his path, but he wouldn't give in. It was too much. Her body was on fire and she twisted in his embrace. He parted her legs and insisted on tasting her there.

"Please. I can't wait."

"You can, love." His tongue found her most sensitive spot and she would have leapt off the bed if he wasn't anchoring her. He used his skill and sensual demands to drive her to new levels of excitement, and when she tightened her grip on his hair, he increased the pressure and she exploded into a powerful climax.

"You're so open." He kissed her inner thigh and smiled at her. Her body was humming with excitement.

He continued a slow exploration of her body, and she touched his chest and moved her hand down to his erection. He closed his hand over hers and guided her into a slow rhythm.

She moved restlessly against him and he positioned himself over her and plunged deeply inside. She held onto his shoulders and let out a gasp.

She could feel pleasure building through her entire body and encouraged each thrust. He captured her nipple with his fingers and she exploded into another release. With one final thrust, he joined her. They lay entwined together, letting their breathing return to normal for several minutes before he got up to discard the condom.

Coming back to bed, he said, "I need you."

She luxuriated in the touch of his embrace and kissed him with all of the desire she was feeling. He pulled her on top of him. She straddled him and responded to his encouragement.

Hours later, she located her clothing and pulled

on her jeans and shirt. Her body was exhausted from the last few hours of intense lovemaking, and she wanted to crawl into his bed and fall asleep. He dressed and insisted on driving her home.

"I can catch the bus. My flat is near a convenient stop."

He pulled her into his arms and kissed her deeply. "I want to take you home."

They silently left the house. He took his silver Porsche and drove through the streets of Dublin at close to three o'clock in the morning.

Glancing out the window, she tried to make sense of her emotions. Her reaction to him was more than physical. She craved a connection to him and could feel herself falling in love. Her steadfast determination to keep their involvement a secret shamed her. Maybe it was because it hurt him in some way? He didn't want to hide what was unfolding between them, but she had insisted. Was it his father and all the torrid secrets that he'd kept that had caused his son to want honesty? Certainly he could see it would only hurt her if they revealed their fling? She was torn between wanting to protect her reputation and wanting to be proud of her relationship with him.

Her head began to pound and she rubbed her temples.

William pulled up near her building. "Are you feeling all right?"

She nodded. "I'm tired. It's late."

Opening the door, she climbed out and waited for him on the sidewalk. "You don't have to walk me up."

He pulled her into his arms. "Goodnight, love. I'll see you tomorrow?"

She hugged him tightly and then kissed him briefly on the lips.

"Goodnight." She walked the few steps to her building and turned when she unlocked the door and saw him watching her pensively. She smiled and stepped inside and ran up the stairs. What was he thinking? Was he surprised by the way the evening unfolded? She should feel regretful, but she didn't in the least.

Chapter 10

William watched Bridget interact with the staff on the small, private plane. She had a friendly demeanor that drew others in. He was getting to understand her on many levels, but preferred the easiness of their relationship when they were alone. In public, he had to be careful not to let down his guard and become too familiar with her. Despite her passionate declaration that she was willing to acknowledge their relationship, in the light of day she continued to insist that they maintain their privacy. Their visit to New York was going to make that difficult. But they had agreed that they would tell their closest friends and family.

It would be impossible to keep a strictly business-only facade at the gala tomorrow evening. The New York social circle looked for gossip and would link their names together. Maybe it would force the issue between them.

The flight attendant disappeared into the front compartment, leaving them alone.

He closed his laptop. "Beyond going to the gala and working in the hotel suite, have you made any plans for the three days?"

She gave him a searching look. "I scheduled a

few appointments with top clients of Breen. I'm hoping to get a sense of how their brand is perceived in New York and if there's any feedback for the company."

He laced his fingers through hers. "I'd like you to join me for dinner each evening. The first is with a few friends and the night after the gala is a few business associates."

She nodded before glancing back at her laptop. "Do you spend much time in New York?"

"I grew up in New York City, but haven't lived there since I was a child. My mother still lives there." He stretched out his legs.

"She must miss you. You're her only child?" Bridget looked at him.

He took a sip of espresso. "She has her own life, and I see her a few times a year."

Glancing back at her laptop, she said, "That's a rather evasive answer."

He formed his hands into a steeple. "My mother isn't the warm, sentimental type. She's organizing the gala that we're attending tomorrow night, so you'll meet her and can form your own opinion."

***

Bridget thought about Diane Bolles. She had looked the socialite up in the media and she was reported to be quite a livewire. She took part in different charity work and was photographed often among the elite New York social world. Would Diane welcome her or simply ignore her? Normally people who traveled in those elite social circles cared about social standing and wealth. Bridget could claim neither.

William met her gaze. "Have you been to New York before?"

She shook her head. "No, I've never been. I'm rather excited. There are so many fashion houses and boutiques. I'll be able to see how Olivia's designs are showcased."

He smiled at her. "We can do whatever you like. Take in a show, walk in Central Park, or go see the fashion houses."

A warmth spread throughout her body. "You're willing to do that? Aren't you the person who said that women may wear a baseball cap as far as you're concerned?"

He smiled. "I've been corrected. By both you and Olivia."

Bridget laughed. "Now you own a hat company."

It was a risk coming to New York. She agreed to come along for personal reasons. She'd visit a few customers for Breen, but those interactions could have taken place over the phone. She wanted to escape with William. They had to be careful in Dublin, but New York would give them much more freedom.

"I have the marketing plan nearly complete for Breen. Can I show you?"

William turned towards her. "Absolutely."

"With your blessing, I'll send it off to the management team."

Opening the file on her laptop, she positioned the screen so he could see and began to discuss the various elements.

She glanced at him and noticed he was watching her, not the presentation. "Have I lost your interest?"

"Definitely not." He touched her thigh and

moved his hand under her skirt.

She let out a playful shriek and tried to push his hand away. "We can't, William."

"We're alone, love." He traced small circles on her leg.

She held his hand still. "There are crew members that could walk through the cabin."

She undid her seatbelt. "I'm going to use the bathroom. Can you glance through the document?"

Standing up, there was a moment of turbulence and William pulled her into his lap. He was a potent combination of playfulness and intensity. He captured her mouth and she kissed him back. Deciding to push his boundaries, she began to unbutton his shirt between kisses.

He stopped her. "Enough. You were right."

She untangled herself from him and headed to the bathroom. It was crazy how happy she felt. Did he feel the same?

The plane landed and a limousine was waiting to take them to the Four Seasons New York. William answered a few calls en route and spoke about different investment opportunities with Alex.

William ended his call and said, "Olivia and Fionn are already in New York. They are coming to the gala tomorrow night. It was a charity my father was involved in, and for the last few years my mother has continued to support it."

She placed a hand over her chest and could feel her heart racing. Olivia would guess that she had something going on with William. "It's going to be an issue for us." She worried that others would judge her for leaping into a fling with her handsome boss.

"We can refuse to answer specific questions and hope that my family doesn't ask too many. But it'll come out."

She nodded. "It was naive of me to think that we could keep it under wraps. It's fine. I'm not ashamed of the relationship, but we will have to figure the professional complexities."

"I took on The Breen Hat Company because you had promised to run it. I don't see that changing. Whatever happens between us will have no impact on that."

Things had a way of working out, didn't they? At least she hoped it would work out. She had used the lucrative sign-on bonus to buy her father a small cottage. But instead of focusing solely on work, she had allowed herself to be drawn into a dream. She thought about her safe, predictable life back in London, and how she tried to refuse Olivia's offer.

She moistened her lips. "What do you think will happen with us?"

He met her gaze. "Do you mean after marriage and three kids?"

She inwardly cringed. Why would she ask him about the future? They had barely started dating and she had no idea what she wanted in the future.

"Just three?"

The driver pulled up to the hotel and helped them with the luggage. Walking into the opulent foyer, her nerves became heightened.

"William, dear." A striking blond woman in her late fifties approached them. Bridget recognized Diane Bolles.

His mother embraced him and said, "I can see you decided to bring a companion."

"Mother, this is Bridget North. She oversees one of my companies in Dublin."

Bridget held out her hand. "It's a pleasure to meet you, Mrs. Bolles."

Diane ignored her outstretched hand and focused her attention on William. "Dublin is a horrible place. You can barely get a decent cup of coffee. Let alone any art or culture."

She let her hand fall and straightened her posture. "I don't know if that's accurate. I grew up in Dublin."

"Poor darling." The woman gave her a pitiful look. Could his mother be any more offensive?

Diane spoke directly to William. "Why don't you put away your things and join me at the bar?"

William placed his arm around her shoulders. "Not tonight, I'm afraid. Bridget and I have plans, but I can meet for lunch tomorrow?"

Bridget didn't look at Diane. She could only imagine how much spite and resentment the woman would be directing towards her.

"I'm too busy to meet you for lunch. I'll see you at the event." Diane walked off without another word.

William led Bridget to the elevator. As the doors closed, she said, "That was unpleasant."

"My mother is tough."

Bridget thought about her own mother. She would give anything to be able to have lunch with her again. Why did Diane not see that demanding things from her only son would not work? Why didn't she make time to see him tomorrow?

Stepping inside the suite one level down from the

penthouse, William pulled her into his arms. "I'm sorry you had to deal with her."

Moving out of his arms, she walked into the spacious well-appointed main room. The furnishings were all in muted shades of grey and reminded her of opulence and luxury. She ran her hand over the soft linen covering the sofa. "I'm fine. I didn't expect her to like me. I can only imagine she would choose someone else for her only son."

William crossed his arms. "Do you mean would she prefer that I date a member of the New York upper class instead of a working class girl from Dublin?"

His bluntness surprised her. "I know the answer and so do you."

He took off his suit jacket and removed his tie. "It doesn't matter to me what she thinks of my life. I've no intention of following in her footsteps. Instead of finding a suitable match, someone she loved, she married the name. That choice hasn't served her well or brought her any real happiness."

Bridget thought of her family growing up. They were of little means, but they were happy. Her mother's sister, who lived in London and took an interest in her, bridged the gap for her family. She was able to provide for her education and take her on trips. Not to mention encouraging a career path that would open up new possibilities for her. Would her aunt be proud of her choice to date William? Or would she cringe? Did it matter what others thought?

She thought about the high-strung socialite. "Do you normally bring the women you date to meet your mother?"

William sat on the sofa and appeared relaxed.

"No. She's not interested in meeting anyone from my life unless the woman happened to have clout in the New York scene. Then she would be interested."

She sat on the sofa close to him. "Why, if you were raised in this environment, do you not care more about finding acceptance here?"

He watched her closely. "New York can be an insane place. Growing up with parents who fought constantly, had shallow friends, and spent way too much time trying to impress others is not a life I wish to return to. It doesn't appeal to me. I much prefer to be out in nature or playing sports."

It was odd to be in New York with him. He seemed so at home in Dublin, it was hard to imagine this was his real home. "But you did take over the Bolles Financial Empire?"

He hesitated for a moment and then said, "Not in the way you think. When my father died unexpectedly, the investment firm was in trouble and had to be closed. Fionn handled the problems and made sure that a set amount of money was placed in trust for me. I could only access it when I turned twenty-five."

"How were you able to build a large company in a few short years?" She looked at him. "That's really impressive."

He crossed his ankles. "I took risks. I launched a small investment group when I graduated college, and used the Bolles name to attract money. Some of the money was invested overseas in mining operations, but I also bought and sold small companies in England and Ireland."

She thought about the delicate balance of realizing great returns and investing into ventures that would fail. "Have you ever taken too many risks?"

William pulled her into his arms. "I don't know if that's possible."

As he kissed her neck, she wondered if their relationship was a risk for him. What type of reward could there be? He devoured her mouth, and any coherent thought left her brain. She craved his touch and wanted to lose herself in him.

***

The next day was a blur of activity. She had arrived back to the hotel in time to take a rushed shower and get ready for the formal gala. Even though she shared a bedroom with William the night before, she placed her clothing in one of the other bedrooms and used the space to get ready. The gown she had brought from London was couture and had been given to her as a bonus for working hours and hours on a last-minute launch.

Working in the fashion business had certain perks. If she had been in another industry, she wouldn't have had something appropriate to wear. It took a serious amount of money to purchase couture. The illusion neckline bodice had a sheer halter top and featured a stunning display of twinkling bejeweled lace. The dress was designed to create curves with striped detailing that draped the full-length hem with glamour.

Adding four-inch stiletto heels and a generous amount of makeup gave her the look she wanted. Grabbing a hairbrush, she managed to create a decent bun with pins and hair gel, when she heard William knock on the door.

She looked up at him through the mirror as he

walked into the room. He took her breath away. He looked polished and masculine in formal attire, and it reminded her of the night they had met a year ago. It was a much different look then his cycling outfit or even a business suit, and he looked impossibly sexy.

"Are you ready?" He sounded slightly impatient, as if he wanted to get the evening over with.

Turning to him, she said, "You look fabulous."

She watched his eyes rake over her and desire settle over him. Instead of seducing her, he turned and walked out of the room. Why was he stressed about going tonight? What wasn't he telling her?

Walking in silence with him to the elevator, she thought about the evening ahead. She was eagerly awaiting the festivities. Working in the fashion world, she had dreamed of coming to New York and attending a black-tie event. She would see firsthand the gowns and accessories worn by the elite social crowd. There would probably be numerous gowns from Olivia's spring line being worn.

"I notice the absence of a hat."

The doors opened and she contemplated answering him. He knew so little about the fashion world. But it wasn't worth an explanation; he wasn't that interested in understanding the nuances of women's clothing.

The event was being hosted in the Four Seasons Hotel so they made their way over to the ballroom. William was stopped several times and he chatted amicably and introduced her. Their photograph was taken a few times in the foyer and William was at ease and stayed by her side.

Attending this event together was announcing to

the socially connected New York scene that they were an item. Why had she thought that she would be able to fade into the background? Apparently the Bolles name drew interest and speculation. It was clear that everyone present knew who William Bolles was and wanted his attention.

A few times she tried to give him space, but he merely anchored her with his arm or held her hand. At one point, he whispered, "Trust me, you don't want to be left alone in this crowd–they will tear you apart."

She observed his mother from afar, but she hadn't spoken to Diane yet tonight. The whole event was a fascinating show of wealth and privilege. She recognized many of the designer gowns and took in all the discussion about fashion. Many acquaintances sought William's advice about the markets, but he mainly suggested that they grab drinks at some point.

He led her onto the dance floor and gathered her into his arms. She was enjoying the event and was surprised to see a strained look on his face.

She asked him, "Has something upset you?"

The memory of their first encounter came back to her. She hadn't known him, but based on his family name, had treated him badly. Had someone this evening slighted him in same way?

He looked into her eyes. "This event reminds me of my father and the good he wanted to do in the world."

What was she missing? "You must come to many events like this one."

William hesitated for a minute, and said, "When he was alive, he started this event and it has continued on. He formed the charity. His idea was to find successful business people that had something to give back and then assign them to a charitable project. By the time I was ten or so, he would bring me to the different locations that benefitted from the funding. I found the formal event horribly boring each year, but I had no idea that he would leave this earth before I could understand the good it did."

Her heart softened. She had been so excited by the fashion aspects of the event that she didn't think about the deeper concerns. "I didn't realize. I'm sorry."

He pulled her closer and she could feel his breath and her body began to heat. "I don't want you to be sorry. It's refreshing that you find joy in this atmosphere. It's exactly what I need tonight."

***

William caught sight of Olivia speaking with a group of people. There had to be more than five hundred guests tonight. Another set of doors had opened and guests were beginning to make their way to the elaborate dinner being offered.

He guided Bridget from the dance floor and they made their way to the front table. The room looked spectacular and the executive director of the charity was on stage.

Fionn and Olivia were seated with them. Bridget greeted them warmly and sat down. His sister was glowing and seemed rather pleased that he and Bridget were an item. He shook Fionn's hand and sat between Bridget and his mother. Diane wouldn't be happy that Bridget had an association with Olivia.

Immediately, his mother whispered to him, "I hadn't realized that Olivia had introduced you to your companion."

"She has a name."

His mother whispered, "Knowing you, she won't be around long enough for me to bother learning it."

He ignored his mother and asked Bridget if she needed anything.

His mother took the stage after the formal speeches and did a plea for more donations.

Olivia and Bridget became lost in discussing the ins and outs of the fashion industry. It seemed that many of the fashion icons were present tonight. William escaped to one of the bar areas with Fionn.

Fionn ordered two Jameson whiskeys and asked him, "How is everything? I know some of your investors are getting cold feet."

No matter how established he became, Fionn would always be a step ahead of him. "There is risk involved in buying and selling companies."

Fionn looked concerned. "What I'm hearing is that The Donne is a sentimental investment and bleeding you dry."

He decided not to allow himself to become defensive. "There is truth to that."

"Why don't you cut your losses?" Fionn looked baffled. He didn't believe in holding on to an investment for sentimental reasons.

"The Donne Resort and Golf Club is close to breaking even. It is going to be named as a destination for one of the major golf events next year."

Fionn adjusted his collar. "Have they signed a contract?"

The bartender handed them each a whiskey and he took a large swallow.

He disliked Fionn checking up on him. He was no longer a kid and could handle his own troubles. "The course needs to be finished before the final commitment is extended. It will happen."

"The timing is getting close. They could select another venue. I don't understand your fascination. Do you plan to name the course for your father?"

He wasn't interested in Fionn's opinion. Fionn had been good to him, but his relationship with Oliver was complex and problematic. "Does it matter?"

"William, if you lose your shirt then it will matter. For better or worse, we are part of a family and your reputation does have an impact on my holdings."

William rubbed the back of his neck. "So you're concerned about your bottom line?"

Fionn placed his drink on the bar. "No. I'm concerned about you. If you need capital, I can help."

He shook his head. "I've liquidated other assets and am moving forward."

His eyes widened. "You've sold your villa in France?"

Why did he feel so defensive? Something had to give if he was going to continue funding The Donne. "I did."

Fionn placed his hand on his shoulder. "At some point, you need to consider London or New York. You can't stay in Ireland forever if you intend to get to the next level. You need to face your adversaries and naysayers in the major markets."

New York would take his soul. London he could deal with. "I have no interest in being in New York or London."

Fionn looked pensive. "The naysayers bother

183

you. That's the central issue. It's not about achieving success, it's about being proud of who you are and where you come from."

William took a swallow of whiskey. "It's about success. Pure and simple." He and Fionn had much different outlooks on life.

"You are no longer a boy, Will. There is more to life than acquiring wealth. I see how you shut down when your father is criticized. Somehow you need to get past that."

William placed his glass on the bar. "It doesn't bother me in the same way anymore."

Fionn held up his hands. "Then why are you risking everything for a golf course that you want to name after him?"

He had been asking himself the same question. "I'm not naming it after him. We played there often and I enjoy the memories. Is that such a problem?"

"It is if you're willing to lose everything. At the end of the day, he's gone."

"There's a newsflash."

Bridget and Olivia joined them and the conversation moved to other topics.

Bridget laced her arm through his and smiled up at him.

Olivia said, "Your mother is in her element. The executive director let us know that the charity did well this evening."

His father's real critics were not here this evening. If he wanted to seek them out then he would need to go elsewhere. Did it matter?

He smiled at his sister. "It's important. How are you feeling?"

"I'm well, but designing the right gown wasn't easy." She ran a hand over her round belly.

They spent several more minutes chatting until Olivia yawned. "I've been tired lately. Especially with travelling."

Olivia and Bridget embraced and then he kissed his sister on the cheek.

Fionn shook his hand saying, "Good luck and let me know if you need help."

He wanted to take Bridget upstairs, but instead he led her back to the dance floor. Fionn had a point: he had to be careful to not cling to the past.

It had been said many times that he was hiding out in Ireland. He didn't see it that way, but it was easier than having to defend the Bolles name. When he returned, he would seek out his brother and, if it was true, he would tell his sisters.

***

On her last day in New York, Bridget was invited to attend a luncheon at Vogue with Olivia. William had left early in the morning for a meeting, and she used the hotel's workout room and then spent time on her computer.

At eleven thirty, she took a shower and dressed in a straight grey skirt with a white silk top. It was a warm summer in New York, so she didn't bother with stockings, but she wore four-inch heels and added a few accessories. In her regular life, she was known as a fashion expert, but it was intimidating coming to New York and having to attend an event with people that were real experts.

Olivia met her in the lobby. "I'm surprised my brother has let you disappear for a few hours."

Bridget laughed. "He has no interest in a lunch at Vogue. He's probably biking around the city."

Olivia looked gorgeous in a silk dress. "Did he bring his bicycle?"

"I think so." She had woken up after he left this morning and there was a cryptic note about escaping the world of suits and ties. It was possible that he was escaping the stress of the financial world by heading off on his bicycle.

"There should be a limousine waiting outside."

The traffic was heavy, and Bridget watched the pedestrians make their way through the crowded streets. New York had a pace that was unbelievable.

"When I first visited New York, I was mesmerized by all the activity."

Bridget turned to Olivia. "I know. I can't believe that I'm here and going to Vogue."

"How are things at The Breen Hat Company?"

"It's been a struggle. Mainly it's the emotional side of the business that's tricky to manage. I understand the marketing and the numbers, but the employees have been living in a stressful and uncertain environment for some time."

Olivia smiled gently. "It's difficult, but I've learned in business that emotions need to be honestly addressed and then put aside."

"The owner, Patrick Breen, has good ideas, but he's exhausted and somewhat unwilling to change. William is ready to replace him, but I'd rather give him more time."

"If you are protecting him from the consequences of his actions, then I don't think it will work."

"It would be a shame to lose the connection to the

past."

"As a manager, you have to be willing to make hard choices or the company could go under. I've seen situations where a change, even if resisted in the beginning, was the best thing for the individual."

The limousine left them off near the building and they were guided into an elaborate luncheon. There were less than fifty guests and they were placed at different tables.

A designer seated near her commented, "I saw your photograph with William Bolles. It was stunning. We're considering using it."

It surprised her, and the conversation turned into an inquiry about where William spent most of his time.

Another woman asked, "Where did the two of you meet?"

"We met through his sister, Olivia Bolles."

The topic switched to the upcoming fashion week. She thought about William deciding not to spend too much time in the New York social scene, and began to understand why.

She and Olivia arrived back at the hotel in the late afternoon.

Olivia said, "Do you want to have tea? I think the men are at a meeting."

Bridget nodded. Did Olivia plan to interrogate her on William's life? Or maybe warn her off from having a romantic relationship?

They were seated in the restaurant, overlooking the lobby, and the forest-like setting soothed her nerves. A waiter took their order and disappeared.

"It's so lovely to have you in New York. When

you went to Breen, I didn't expect to see you for a year. You're very much missed at the studio."

"It's been a transition, for sure. I didn't expect to be back in Dublin, and I miss everyone terribly."

The waiter returned and served a pot of tea.

"William said that your father lives near the golf course and that you see him often?"

"We used to talk on the phone all the time, but I would only get home twice a year. Now I see him a couple of times a week. He's living outside of Dublin, and I found a flat near Breen."

Olivia took a sip of her tea. "It sounds lovely. Do you have any thoughts on what will happen when the year is over?"

"I plan on returning to London." How could she not? Her relationship with William would end well before the year was up and she would be counting the weeks. He wasn't into long-term relationships.

Olivia smiled at her. "But you seem to be crazy about my brother."

"I am, but I realize that it was foolish to jump into a relationship with someone I work for. It's not something I'm proud of."

Olivia touched her hand. "Bridget, love can happen. It's impossible to plan, and from what I can tell, you're both unattached adults. So I wouldn't be apologetic about it. Enjoy each other."

She wasn't sure how to respond, so she changed the subject. "Can you tell me what's happening at the studio?"

Olivia smiled and then launched into a discussion of the plans for Fashion Week and the new collection.

William and Fionn joined them a short while later

and they said their goodbyes. Getting onto the elevator with William, she couldn't wait to be alone with him. This would be their last evening in New York, and she wanted to make the most of it.

They were expected out in an hour, but spent most of it entwined in each other's arms until she insisted they spend a few minutes getting ready.

The dinner that evening was in the Gramercy Tavern's private dining room.

Bridget showered in minutes and put on one of the couture black dresses she brought with her. She could hear William call out that he was ready. Putting on sheer black stockings, she slipped her feet into Italian heels and then went in search of earrings. Her face was flushed, so she added a touch of mascara and put her hair up in a messy updo.

They arrived a few minutes late and were shown to the private dining room. William kept his hand on her lower back and drew her closer when he introduced her to a dozen or more business contacts. The room was an intimate space with a single, grand table set beneath a wood-beamed ceiling with elegant chandeliers. They joined the others standing about having cocktails.

Watching him entertain various couples with stories of skiing in Switzerland and biking in Tanzania, she recalled the comments by a Vogue editor. William was recognized and sought after in New York. Was it possible that he worried too much about others disparaging his father? The scandals were years ago, and she couldn't imagine that many people could hold a grudge for that long.

One of the women asked her where she had met

William, and she explained it was through his sister.

All twenty people drew a slip of paper from a glass bowl and were asked to match the image to a place setting at the table. Her image was a bluebird and she took a seat near the end of the table. An advertising executive was seated to her left and a vice president of an investment brokerage to her right. Waiters came out and served a beet salad with almonds, fregola, and Asian pear for the appetizer.

"Do you model, Ms. North?" the gentleman to her right asked.

"Bridget, please. I work in fashion. For the last few years, I've done the marketing for Olivia Bolles Designs, but I've recently shifted to managing The Breen Hat Company in Dublin."

"I've not heard of Breen. Do you enjoy the work?"

"It's exhausting at the moment, but also exhilarating."

The conversation continued for some time and a waiter came around and poured wine. The conversation around the table flowed easily and Bridget was welcomed into the banter. She could feel herself relax and absorb the interesting ideas and discussions around her.

The woman to her left said, "It's unfortunate about William. He could have done great things."

"What do you mean?"

"The Bolles name will always weigh him down."

"I don't agree with you. There's a new generation, and they are all rather successful and talented."

The next course was served and she enjoyed the

delicious soup.

The woman's voice held a trace of disdain. "Yes, but he can't escape his father's legacy."

Bridget smiled and said, "I attended a gala last night for homeless and disadvantaged youth. Oliver Bolles had started the fundraiser."

The woman took a sip of her wine. "He was a saint, wasn't he?" The disdain in the woman's voice was surprising. She must have had a negative interaction with Oliver.

She needed to be careful, but couldn't allow the comment to pass. "No. I don't think he was a saint. He was human and made mistakes. William loved him, but was aware of his flaws."

The subject around the table changed to politics and the conversation drifted to other topics.

After nearly two hours and five courses, the meal ended and people slowly left the table and milled about the room.

William was talking with a blonde wearing a short red dress who had wrapped her body around his arm. Instead of holding back, she walked up to them and introduced herself to the blonde.

The blonde said, "Would you give us a few minutes? I have something of a personal nature to discuss with William."

Bridget looked at William, who unwrapped himself and said, "Your finances are hardly of a personal nature, Elaine. Why don't you chat with Bridget? I have to have a word with someone."

He kissed her cheek and whispered, "I won't be long."

The woman pouted. "How did you entice him

into dating? I've tried for years, and he's always been more interested in triathlons and outdoor adventures."

"He does appreciate the outdoors."

She glanced at William and noticed he was speaking with the host of the event. She asked her companion, "Do you know who William is speaking to?"

"Walter Brown. He owns a large investment firm."

She nodded. "The financial world in New York is a mystery to me."

"You have a drop-dead gorgeous dress."

She smiled at the woman. She was friendly and harmless, even if she would like to dig her nails into William.

They talked a few more minutes until William joined them and said, "We must be going."

They said goodnight to Elaine and politely excused themselves. Saying goodbye to everyone on the way out, he held her hand tightly until they were on the street.

William pulled her into an embrace. "It's only a few blocks. Can you walk?"

She laughed. "Maybe."

"You look amazing, but wouldn't you rather be comfortable?"

She gave him a quizzical look. "My clothing fits well and is comfortable, but the shoes are meant for hard surfaces, not rough terrain or grass."

"Did you enjoy yourself tonight?"

"I was placed near interesting people and the food was superb. How about you?"

"Being in New York is challenging because

everyone has an opinion about the Bolles family."

She listened quietly and he continued, "I spoke with Walter Brown. He's interested in funding a new project. It could lead to the establishment of a London office."

She thought about the complexities of the financial world in New York. William seemed to manage all of it. Olivia had made a throwaway comment about William needing to base himself in London or New York. Would he choose London? If they were both going to base themselves in London in the future, did it mean that their relationship might survive? Even though she was trying to hold herself back, she was becoming more and more attached to him with each passing day.

Chapter 11

The small jet landed late at a private airport outside of Dublin. Bridget had enjoyed hours of conversation with William during the flight. The three days spent in New York were such a whirlwind that they had tons to discuss.

She had been living a fantasy. Instead of worrying about her relationship with William, they had been open about it and photographed often. The nights had been pure pleasure, and Bridget didn't want to separate from him.

Climbing down the plane's staircase, William stopped at the bottom and took her in his arms. "Come home with me."

She wanted to keep up the pretense about their relationship now that they were back in Dublin. It was one thing for Olivia and his mother to know, but quite another for the people they worked with to know.

Bridget clung to him and whispered, "I don't think that's a good idea."

He pulled back and looked at her. "We're in a relationship, and to hide that feels wrong."

"I'm tired and the work week starts in a few hours. It would be better if we each go home and talk later in the day."

"Sure." He led her over to his Range Rover and, after the crew brought over their luggage, they drove the short distance to Dublin.

She was handling this all wrong. "I don't know how to navigate all of this."

His jaw clenched and he said, "Playing the helpless girlfriend doesn't reflect well on you. You are adept at handling a variety of situations. The issue is that you don't want to deal with it."

What could he possibly mean by handling situations? "We've talked about this. My career is important to me. I need to be able to support myself and help my father. I can't throw it away on a romantic fling."

"I'm not asking you to throw anything away. I'm asking you to be honest about it."

What did he possibly know about starting from nothing? "William, you grew up in privilege and never had to worry about your reputation."

His hands tightened on the steering wheel. "The fact that my father led a double life, was rumored to steal from his investors, and had numerous children with other women guaranteed that I grew up with a shadow following me everywhere."

She hadn't thought of it in those terms. "In New York, people couldn't get enough of you. You are highly sought- after and you seem to have a flawless reputation."

He slowed down for a light. "I've worked hard to create a positive reputation, but you were only around people who would overlook my family's shortcomings. You weren't exposed to those who would like to see me destroyed."

He reminded her of a golden boy. Everything he touched turned to gold. "I can't imagine there are people who would want to see you destroyed."

His shoulders and neck held visible tension. "You were one of those people. There are hundreds more."

"I'm sorry." He was right. She had cast stones without really knowing who he was and what he stood for.

"I can't pretend that there's nothing between us. It'd be better to stop before it becomes problematic."

Shock washed over her. That was not what she meant. She didn't want to end their relationship before it got properly started. But it was complex and created numerous issues for them.

"I don't want to end our relationship, William. I wanted to find a way to balance our right to some privacy with what we want to share with the outside world."

He downshifted and stopped for another light. "It doesn't work that way. Either you're willing to stand behind your choices or you're not."

"It's one o'clock in the morning, and we're both tired. Can we discuss this tomorrow?"

He remained silent and she looked out the window. Her heart felt like it was shattering into tiny pieces. She had handled the entire situation badly. She ought to consider his viewpoint, but it was nearly impossible for her to trust that everything would work out. He physically craved a connection to her, but hadn't said how he felt about her. How could she possibly take a risk when she had no idea of how he felt?

If she were to tell him the truth right now, she

would have to admit that she was in love with him. But how could that be? They had been seeing each other for less than a few weeks. She was setting herself up for heartbreak.

He double-parked and helped her with her luggage.

"Do you have your keys?" he asked.

She nodded and he said, "Goodnight, love," and turned away from her without kissing her.

She stood on the sidewalk for a few moments watching his vehicle disappear down the dark street. She had offended him. She pushed him away and worried that he wouldn't let her back in. Their trip had been so wonderful. Why did it have to end this way? What was she so afraid of?

   ***

The next morning, William went for a thirty-mile grueling ride at dawn. Getting back to his house before breakfast, he stood at the gate drenched in sweat and depleted, but no closer to understanding Bridget. How could she be so open and caring in private and then shut down in public? He had thought their time in New York had proven to her that they could manage a professional and personal relationship. But she had not softened her stance. He couldn't accept a secret relationship. He was not his father. He would not hide the truth.

His heart was pounding. He put away his bicycle. It hit him that he had put off meeting his brother for weeks so he wouldn't have to deal with the ramifications. That would stop today. He would seek out the woman and her son.

He called to Mary as he walked into the house.

Coming out of the kitchen, she said, "Bridget is here. Are you wanting breakfast?"

"No. I plan to be away for a few days. Could you pack a bag? I don't need suits. Casual and some biking gear is fine."

Mary said, "Bridget is in the kitchen. I'll go and pack."

"I'll shower first. Can you keep her company for a few minutes?" He had expected her to go to Breen today and throw herself into work. Why would she decide to come here?

He stripped off his sweaty shirt and headed to his room. He wasn't feeling calm or controlled. How was she able to mess with his head so easily?

Getting out of the shower, he dried off and dressed in jeans and a cycling shirt. The water had done nothing to soothe his nerves. He never allowed his emotions to overtake him, but right now he had the desire to fight with Bridget. He would refuse to back down, and the relationship would be over. Maybe that was for the best?

Stepping into the kitchen, he saw her leaning against the counter and chatting with his housekeeper. Her fitted dress and narrow belt highlighted her slim build perfectly. A fierce desire burned through him and he ruthlessly pushed it away.

***

Bridget gazed at the open doorway and saw William watching her. Her heart squeezed in her chest. It had only been a few hours, yet she had missed him terribly.

Mary dried her hands on her apron and said, "I'll go and pack."

William stepped into the room, and she could feel the tension radiating from his body.

"I'm sorry, William. It was wrong of me to insist that nothing change between us."

A silence descended on the room. He was not going to accept her apology.

He crossed his arms. "I don't think a relationship between us will work. I want complete transparency and you need complete privacy. Trying to continually negotiate it will only lead to arguments and hurt feelings."

She stepped towards him. Would he turn her down? "I'm willing to go for complete transparency. I'd rather risk my reputation than risk my relationship with you." Could she risk her heart and survive the heartbreak if he decided he didn't want to give it a try?

His head jerked back. "You're willing to admit to a relationship with me?"

She nodded and waited for his response.

He picked her up and spun her around. Slowly lowering her in his arms, he kissed her deeply. A feeling of breathlessness overtook her as her mind made sense of his reaction. He wanted the relationship. The risk no longer held any power over her. Happiness bubbled up inside her, and she touched the flat surface of his chest and returned his kiss.

He held her in his arms. "I'm taking a few days and driving down to meet my brother. Can you come with me?"

She looked away. "We've been in New York. I need to get back to Breen."

"I'll send Jeremy, and you can check in by phone."

She thought about it. She should put work first, but William needed her. Meeting his brother was going to be emotional.

Pushing aside her doubts, she said, "All right. I'll need to stop at my flat."

* * *

Packing the Range Rover with cycling equipment, he asked Bridget to send a message to the management team that they would be travelling for a couple of days and would reach out to them later in the week. They had a four-hour drive south ahead of them, and had his assistant book lodging near a well-regarded touring area.

It crossed his mind that for someone who harped on openness, he was being somewhat mysterious. But he needed to find out who these people were before involving his sisters. Once the media got wind of it, there would be a firestorm of speculation.

He opened the door to the Range Rover for Bridget, but before she could climb in, he took her in his arms and kissed her. He craved her, and it worried him. He wanted her along on this journey, which was odd for him. He usually handled these type of things alone.

They drove to her flat and he waited in the car for her to pack. Turning off his phone, he listened to La Bohème and tried to dispel images of the last time he had seen his father. Did his father know that he would have another child? He could be walking into a situation that could plague him for the rest of his life or bring him enormous joy.

When Bridget retuned with her bag, he got out and placed it in the back seat.

"So we're also having a cycling adventure?"

"We can't surprise them and then expect to spend the entire day with them."

Bridget turned towards him. "They don't know that you're coming?"

"I decided this morning, but my attorney sent a letter three weeks ago."

***

After an uneventful drive, they knocked on a small wooden door to a stone cottage. The entire property looked like it belonged in the nineteenth century.

William had the feeling that his father was with him. He ran a hand through his hair and pushed away the anger that coursed through his body. Why would his father be so careless?

A striking yet frail-looking woman with muted red hair and deep blue eyes opened the door. "Can I help you?"

He had expected her to look sickly. "I'm William Bolles and this is Bridget North."

The woman paled and looked them over. "Please come in. Oliver is not home, but will be in an hour or so. I'm Meredith."

It was odd to hear of another Bolles being called Oliver. He had barely gotten over his sister, Anna, naming her infant son Oliver.

His thoughts were hazy, but he could feel Bridget's hand on his arm, anchoring him in the present. Meredith was different from his own mother. She was charming, but didn't enhance her looks, instead seemed to play them down. Their house was so modest that he was ashamed of his father for not providing for them. The furniture was old and cheap. His father's choices were odd. The women he chose to have a relationship with were vastly different. Had this woman been the love of his life?

He wanted to escape from the tiny house but forced himself to remain. "I apologize for intruding, but couldn't wait any longer. My attorney had sent you some paperwork, but it hadn't been returned yet."

"I've been recovering for the last few months, and haven't been able to get to everything."

"Please don't worry," Bridget said kindly.

Meredith moved about the kitchen and put on water for tea.

Bridget gently ushered him over to the pine table and pulled out a chair for him and then sat down next to him.

Meredith served them scalding hot tea, taking a seat opposite them at the table. He decided not to ask about her illness. It was better to let her disclose information.

He kept his voice low and respectful. "I'm renovating The Donne Golf Resort and a few of the locals told me that you were in love with my father. It was widely known that when he died tragically you were carrying his child. Why didn't you approach the family for help?"

She folded her hands. "It was a long time ago." She looked away for a brief time, then looked at him. "What are your plans for Oliver?"

What could he possibly say? They were going to be at odds. They were from different social and economic worlds. "I'm curious about him. I'd like to spend some time with him and find out if he is interested in a establishing a relationship."

Meredith's voice hesitated. "He's a good boy. He does well in school and likes football. But not having a family has been hard for him, especially when I got sick a year ago."

"I'm sorry." Bridget reached across the table and took Meredith's small hand in hers.

"I'm recovering, but during my hospitalizations, Oliver had to take a year off from school."

William sipped his tea and listened to her. She had dedicated her life to her only son and worried that she wouldn't be around to guide or encourage him. He stopped himself from offering to take Oliver under his wing. It would be up to his brother.

He heard the door open and a young man call out, "Mama, I'm home."

William stood up and came face-to-face with a younger version of himself. It was unmistakable. He was a Bolles. They could do sophisticated DNA testing, but it wouldn't matter.

The boy held out his hand and said, "I'm Meredith's son, Oliver Barrett."

He shook his hand and said, "I'm your brother, William Bolles."

The teenager became still and the color drained from his face.

His mother went over and led him to the table. "I know it is a shock to meet your brother in this way. This is his friend, Bridget."

He held out his hand to Bridget.

Oliver looked at him and said, "I never met my biological father. With all due respect, I don't know what you want from us."

Meredith interrupted. "It's not about wanting anything. It's about getting to know your father's family. You've a brother and two sisters."

Oliver looked at his mother. "It's always been you and I. We don't need other people in our lives."

He understood the boy's reluctance to open himself up. He was at a difficult age. It was the age he was when his father died.

"Oliver, I know the entire situation is awkward. You can treat me like an acquaintance or a distant family friend."

Oliver shrugged. "Fine."

"Meredith, are you well enough to come out for dinner this evening?"

Meredith nodded. "I'm on the mend and can certainly have dinner."

Oliver met his gaze. "I don't want to have dinner and pretend this is normal. It'd be better if you said what you came to say and then left."

"I'm not expecting you to be overjoyed at the prospect of having an older brother. It'll take time to get to know each other. But doing small things, such as sharing a meal or going for a walk will make this process more bearable."

"You haven't said what you want from us."

This kid was impossible. "I want a younger brother. Someone who will kick the football around or go on an adventure with me."

"I used to want that when I was a little boy, but now that I'm seventeen, I'm not interested."

He stood up. "I'll see you at dinner. Thank you, Meredith."

He heard Bridget say goodbye and could feel her arm linked with his as they walked outside.

Walking back to his Range Rover, images of his father assaulted him. He would need to relocate to London for a period of time if he was going to help Oliver get into a university and rebuild his family's legacy. Eventually his brother would take on the Bolles name and he wouldn't allow the media to make his brother's life difficult.

***

William was quiet on the ride back to the hotel. It must have been odd to come face-to-face with someone who clearly shared the same genetic background. It was uncanny how similar the two looked.

William parked the Range Rover. "Do you want to relax at the hotel or go for a ride?"

"I'll go for a ride."

After checking in and changing into their cycling clothes, they went outside and he took her bike off the vehicle. William went over the bicycle and then pointed for her to get the helmets while he took his bicycle off the vehicle.

"Do you have the route mapped out?" Was he planning to do an insane amount of kilometers?

He put his helmet on. "I found a few different routes. Why don't we start and see what happens? We only have two hours if we are going to make it back in time to have dinner with Meredith and Oliver."

Bridget lost all sense of time as she followed him through the winding roads. The area had rolling hills and pristine forests and was much more rural than she first realized.

William set an intense pace, and Bridget pushed herself to keep up with him. She thought about his family and how amazing it was to have siblings. Oliver would be a welcome addition to the Bolles clan. She could imagine how much love and attention his sisters would lavish on him. And William would take the boy under his wing.

Had he spoken with them already? In New York, Olivia hadn't mentioned anything.

She had a couple of messages from Breen on her phone and she needed to throw herself back into work.

The hotel came into sight, and she pushed herself to pass William. He caught up to her near the Range Rover and said, "You're amazing on a bicycle."

"I'm surprised we didn't use the entire two-hour block of time."

William climbed off of his bike. "I have a different activity planned for us."

She laughed. "I have a few work calls to make." Stepping off the bicycle, her legs could barely support her.

"The hills were intense."

After dealing with the equipment, he pulled her into his arms and kissed her provocatively. "You should put off the calls."

She could feel his hard body against hers and she didn't have a chance. "Let's go."

An hour later at the restaurant, they waited for Meredith and Oliver in the foyer. She could barely take her eyes off of William. The last hour between them had been raw and intense. He had wanted to pleasure her and didn't stop until she was satiated and limp.

He held her hand. "I can't wait to get this dinner over with and have you all to myself again."

How could she have thought that they shouldn't spend every night together? She would miss him when he traveled next.

Meredith and Oliver arrived and they stepped forward to greet them.

William signaled the host and they were shown to a private table.

"Thank you for inviting us, William."

"It's my pleasure." He took a look at the menu.

Bridget said, "We went for a bike ride this afternoon and the area is unspoiled and pristine. Spending so much time in London and now Dublin, the rolling hills and forests are majestic."

"I came to this area when I was pregnant with Oliver. It was a magical place to raise a little boy. Now that he will be going off to university, it's far from everywhere."

"Maybe I can convince you both to stay with me when you look at schools in Dublin. I live in a converted pub and there is a ton of space."

Meredith smiled. "That would be lovely."

The waiter took their order and their conversation stayed carefree and easy.

***

Much later, when they were walking out of the restaurant, William said, "We're staying another day, if you have time tomorrow."

"Oliver has school, but I'll be home if you want to come over for tea."

William shook his brother's hand and then gently hugged Meredith. Bridget did the same and they watched the mother and son walk to their car.

"They're both lovely."

William took her hand and they walked back to the hotel.

"I'll have to tell my sisters in the next few days."

She looked at him. "Why haven't you?" Was he afraid of their reaction?

He shook his head. "I've been waiting to confirm a few things with a local attorney."

"Oliver is you. How could you think for a moment that he is not your brother?"

"These things can be complicated. It's smart to be careful."

He was a man of integrity, clearly intending to help his estranged brother. Revealing a weakness was not something that came easily to him. But he'd allowed her to have a front-row seat for the emotional meeting with his brother. Maybe they had a chance at making their relationship work.

Chapter 12

Bridget woke up on Friday morning entangled in William's arms. Struggling to pull the sheet out from under her, she glanced at her phone. It was six o'clock in the morning. They were flying to London that evening, but she needed to spend the day at Breen. The company was devouring all of her energy and time, but it was starting to turn around. She lightly kissed William on his lips and he groaned.

He had not given her any assurances about the future. Taking a shower, she mentally went through her day and began to plan out what she could accomplish and what needed to wait. Stepping out of the shower, she dried off and went back into the bedroom.

William had woken up and was watching her intently.

"I'm needed at Breen this morning."

His voice was rough and insistent. "I need you more."

"Funny. But you have things to do, as we're flying to London tonight."

He propelled himself out of bed and walked naked over to her. "Your loss."

She gave him a surprised look and went in search

of her clothing. She had packed a bag two nights ago. She dressed in a stylish light tweed business dress with a narrow black belt and gathered her laptop and files.

***

They flew in his plane to London that evening. A hired car was waiting at the private airstrip to take them into the city.

"It's odd to be here after two months. So much has changed between us," Bridget said, walking in behind him to his London flat.

"I was fascinated by you from the moment you got off the ferry."

She placed her handbag on the entry table. "Didn't you hold a grudge from our first meeting?" Her heels clicked on the wooden floor.

"I couldn't. You broke down all of my defenses." He placed their luggage in the living room.

Pulling her into his arms, he kissed her. Pure pleasure swept through her and she clung to him.

He picked her up and carried her through the flat.

She held onto his shoulders. "I didn't see your bedroom the last time I was here." It was fun to be carried by him. He was strong and lifted her effortlessly.

"I'd have given you a tour if you had asked."

"I seem to remember you were all business that night," she said teasingly.

He placed her on the bed and came down on top of her. "It was an act."

He unbuttoned his shirt and took it off. She ran her hands over his tightly sculpted chest and he let out a groan.

He kissed her neck and pulled her body closer to

his. "You're wearing too many clothes."

Running his hand down her leg, he removed one shoe and then the other. His hands glided over her thighs and undid her stockings.

Bridget stood and removed the belt from her dress and turned so he would undo the zipper.

His mobile rang and he cursed. Glancing at it, he said, "My mother texted and advised that I turn on the local news. How does she even know that I'm in London?"

He turned on the television and went in search of his laptop.

Bridget watched in shock. William and Oliver's pictures were displayed next to each other and the reporter was commenting on past scandals that impacted the Bolles family. It didn't make sense; how could the media possibly know about his younger brother? They had come to London so he could share the news with his sisters.

William walked back in the room as the reporter said that a person close to the family tipped off the London press. Sitting in a chair near the bed, he scanned articles on the Internet.

"I need to get in touch with the attorney that's handling the investigation. Meredith and Oliver are going to need some advice in handling this situation."

"It's horrible."

"You should get some sleep. I'm going to call my sisters, then get in touch with my attorney." He disappeared and she went in search of her suitcase.

Bridget climbed into bed nearly an hour later after taking a hot bath and giving her aunt a call. Exhaustion claimed her, and she didn't wake up until sunlight was pouring through the windows. Stretching, she wondered why William wasn't in bed.

She could hear raised voices and got up to get dressed.

A few minutes later, she found William sitting alone in the living room. He had showered and was wearing dress pants with a pressed button-down shirt.

"Bridget."

Her heart constricted and she wanted to throw herself into his arms, but something held her back. He was cold and distant.

"I hope you slept well."

"I did." There was a politeness coming from him that worried her. Was he angry with her?

William said, "We need to talk."

A nervous tension was winding its way through her body. He was all business without any softening or playfulness. She could see rejection in every line of his body. He was going to end their relationship.

Sitting down, she smoothed the sleeveless dress over her legs. She had fallen in love with him, and yet her world was about to end.

"I've decided to move my office to London for the foreseeable future. Your work life can remain in Dublin for the next nine months, and then you'll have the opportunity to return to London to look for work." His announcement shattered her heart, but she wasn't going to let him see her fall apart. Instead, she would hide her reaction and pretend everything was fine.

She stood up. "Why are you doing this?"

"My mother was here this morning. She found out you were the one to let the story leak about my brother to a London newspaper."

She held her hands up. "That's not true. I'd never do such a thing."

His eyes were cold and assessing. "I have access to your banking records. I've already confirmed that a large deposit was made into your personal account two days ago from the same London media group that publicized the story."

She stood up. "There has to be some mistake. I did not give the story to the press or accept any money. I wouldn't do that."

His eyes were downcast. "Then why is the payment in your account?"

Why didn't he believe her? "I don't know. It doesn't make any sense. Maybe someone is trying to make trouble for us?"

"It'd be best if you gathered your things and returned to Dublin. It will give me time to sort out everything with my sisters. "

She kept her voice neutral and didn't look at him. "I don't understand. I thought we were happy."

He didn't move. "I thought I could trust you."

She promised herself that she wouldn't plead or grovel. "So...you're going to believe that I did this horrible thing and not let me get to the truth?" Her voice sounded high and uncertain.

He stood up. "I can't function without trust."

He wasn't giving her the opportunity to prove her innocence. He was more than willing to believe the worst of her. Why would someone go through all the effort of making her look guilty?

Her heart felt like it was shattering into a million pieces. "There has to be a way that I can prove to you that it wasn't me. I was set up."

He crossed his arms. "I grew up with deception. I've never understood why anyone would go through such insane lengths to avoid the truth. You can just tell me that you thought the truth should come out."

She held his gaze and knew that he wouldn't offer her another chance.

"I'm not going to admit to something I didn't do. At some point you'll realize that you are wrong, but it will be too late for us." She stepped away from him. "Good luck, William."

He studied her for a moment. "I wish you luck as well."

He left the room and she wiped away a few tears. She had to stop herself from crying here. At home, later, would be the time to fall apart. In truth, she was in shock. Her body felt cold, and she couldn't quite accept that it was over. She expected him to walk back in and take her in his arms. If he cared anything for her, he would do that and not expect her to walk away. Why didn't he realize in his heart that she would never be capable of deceiving him? If he cared for her at all he would know that.

She went through the motions of gathering her things and then hailed a taxi. Why was this happening to her?

Chapter 13

William stood at the edge of the square mile in the financial district of London reflecting on his next move. In the last six weeks, he established a premier office space for Bolles Investments, hired five employees, and convinced investors to place one hundred million with his firm. The amount was set to quadruple in the next quarter. The media had been drawn to his story, and he had been portrayed as the golden boy of finance.

So why was he barely functioning and a shadow of himself? He had faced his fears and his so-called enemies had melted away into nothing. It had been long enough since his father's death that the elite brokers and power investors were ready to move on. They were ready to get behind someone new.

The elite social events and dinners had women throwing themselves at him. But he could barely dance with another woman without feeling his heart constrict. He craved Bridget with an insatiable hunger that was beyond his ability to control. He had accused her of horrible things and thrown her out.

But his sisters wouldn't leave the issue alone. Olivia insisted Bridget was innocent and confided in him that his mother had caused problems between her

215

and Fionn. It had come down to jealousy and she had almost succeeded in keeping them apart. Olivia demanded that he look deeper and find out who spoke with the paper. Anna had called as well to show her concern and let him know that she believed in Bridget.

After six weeks, he finally had the proof that Bridget had been set up. How could he possibly fix it? Why would she forgive him? He shouldn't have needed to proof to know that she was not capable of hurting him.

He had been wrong about her. She had been afraid of taking risks and compromising her reputation. Now it was surely destroyed. How could he have believed that she was capable of selling him out? It had been six weeks, and she probably hated him.

William straightened his tie and crossed the street. He would book his private jet for a flight back to Ireland. He needed her. Even if he had to win her heart all over again.

***

Bridget finished at Breen for the day. She hurried home to change into her bike shorts and reflective shirt to go for a night ride. The exercise had become part of her daily attempt to purge her sadness about William. He hadn't called her since she left London, but his successful debut had been celebrated in the weekly management meetings. The other members of his team hadn't pried into their relationship. Instead they gave her space and encouraged her to keep an open mind about everything.

Filling up her water bottle in the kitchen sink, she heard her buzzer sound. It was odd. Her father normally didn't drop by and she couldn't think of anyone else who would.

She pressed the buzzer. "Hello?"

"Hello yourself."

William. Why would he be here? "What do you want?"

"I need to see you, love. Please." His voice shattered the shell she had built around herself.

She couldn't go through another emotional conversation with him. She'd fall apart. "I think you said everything that there was to say."

"No, I haven't and I'm prepared to wait all evening."

"Come up." She pressed the release button.

She opened the door and waited for him to come up the stairs.

He walked into her flat and her heart constricted. It was crazy, she missed him.

She turned away from him. "I can't imagine that we have anything to say to one another."

A silence spread out between them. She turned back and looked at him. He looked thin. Even though he found commercial success in London, he didn't look happy.

"I'm sorry, Bridget. From the bottom of my heart. I was completely wrong."

"I know that you were wrong." Bridget crossed her arms over her chest. "But your apology means nothing to me. You may believe me now, but the next time your bitter mother decides to frame me, it'll be the same."

He ran a hand through his hair. "It was a despicable thing for her to do."

"I agree." She turned away from him.

"I've learned my lesson. I should have known that you weren't capable of such deceit. I don't know why I was so ready to believe the worst."

She wiped away a few tears. "I do. You are not interested in a deep relationship. If things start to get hard then you look for an excuse to end it."

He reached out and pulled her into arms. "I'm interested in a deep relationship with you. Only you."

She pushed against his chest. "Please don't."

He lightly touched her cheek. "Please forgive me. I have something much more important to say to you, but I can't say it until you forgive me."

She stood up straighter. "I forgive you, William, but that doesn't mean that I want you in my life."

The color drained from his face. "I want you in my life. Forever. Would you marry me?"

He hadn't even told her how he felt. "Marriage is not the answer."

"I love you. I love you with my whole heart. I know I messed up. I intend to spend the rest of my life proving to you that I am trustworthy and loyal."

She touched her throat. "I love you too." Tears began sliding down her cheeks.

"What's wrong, love?"

"Nothing. It's just I missed you so much. I can't believe that you're here and asking me to marry you."

He gently wiped away her tears. "Will you marry me?"

"Yes."

He picked her up and swung her around in excitement.

"Do you want to go and tell your father?"

"No. Right now, I want you all to myself." She

held him tightly. She couldn't believe that he came back. It was what she'd wished for every night. He searched for the truth and came back to her. But it would take a huge leap of faith to believe in him. Could she believe in him?

"I love you, Bridget North. I've loved you since our first meeting when you told me off."

"How is that possible?"

"I don't know. I've held you in my heart since that moment. Someone I knew that you were the one for me. It took me a while to believe it. It took my losing you to know what a fool I've been. I'll never doubt you again."

She reached up and kissed him with all the pent-up longing that she had pushed away. She loved him with a fierceness that surprised her.

"I'll never doubt you, either."

Acknowledgments

It takes a team working together to take a manuscript and produce a compelling novel. I have several people to thank for their hard work, dedication and encouragement along this journey. Getting the story to the reader makes the entire struggle worth it!

To **Erica Monroe**, your powerful feedback and willingness to delve into the fray helped me see things in a much different way. I'll forever be grateful for your kind words of wisdom while insisting that I could 'dig deeper'. You have the discerning quality to not only see someone's strengths and weaknesses but to know how to communicate it to them. I've become a much better writer for it.

To **Stephanie Kay**, your smart critiques and encouragement helped me to keep going. I can't thank you enough for reading this novel twice and catching all sorts of omissions and errors.

To **Meghan Hogue**, your editing skills and insight helped turn this story into a polished novel. It's been wonderful to work with a professional who can see the bigger picture yet fix the small problems.

To **Kim Killion**, your creative genius in cover design and overall professionalism make you an absolute pleasure to work with. Thank you for another amazing cover!

To **Christina Tetreault**, your steadfast loyalty and support made me believe that I could succeed as a writer. Even on the hardest days, I could reach out to you for assistance. Your knowledge and expertise in self-publishing is second to none. I hope we share many more writing adventures together.

To the **members of RWA**, including all of the writers who have joyously shared their craft, I can't thank you enough for sharing your ideas, inspiration and words of wisdom. I'd like to particularly thank **Bob Mayer, Kristan Higgins, Virginia Kantra and Angela James** for their amazing workshops.

To **my children**, for always being proud of me and trying not to interrupt too many times.

To **my husband**, **David**, for your endless support and your eagerness to tell people that you are the inspiration behind the ideas.

And to **my readers**, thank you for taking a chance on this novel. I hope you enjoy it immensely!

Thank You for Reading

Thank you so much for reading *The Chosen Heir*! I hope you enjoyed the story. It would be amazing if you could take a few minutes to review this book on Amazon – your feedback is quite valuable.

Stay in Touch

I love to hear from readers and answer every email personally. Please visit my website, www.susiewarren.com, to sign up for my newsletter and a chance to read my next book early, receive information on discounted prices and free books!

Susie Warren

The Next Book in this Series:

The Sheltered Heiress
His desire for revenge is complicated...

Felix Goldman is a self-made billionaire, admired for his design aesthetic, bold choices, and defending the underdog. But his success hides a core need for revenge. Years ago, the Bolles family destroyed his mother, shattering his childhood and sense of safety. Slowly, he amasses enough wealth to destroy the Bolles's flagship company–and the legacy of unfairness they've left behind. So close to achieving his ultimate goal, Felix didn't count on Grace Bolles, or the simmering attraction he'd feel for her.

By falling in love with her.

Grace Bolles lives a careful existence pursuing her artistic endeavors, never letting anyone get too close to her. A chance encounter with the charming Felix Goldman makes her wonder if she's been missing out on life's greatest pleasures–but when she discovers he plans to destroy her company and legacy, she's forced to decide between their growing attraction and her deep sense of self-protection.

Will her love be enough to lead him down a different path, or will his plan for revenge destroy them both?